THE KISSING TUTOR

SALLY HENSON

Cover design by Victorine Leiske

Content editing by Cara Seger

Editing by Walk the Line Editing & Proofreading

Interior formatting by Sally at Dirt Road Press

CONTENTS

I jogged across the field to the dugout. Tears brimmed, but I refused to let them fall. Not here. Not in front of Coach or my teammates.

Sweat dripped down my forehead. I swiped it with the back of my wrist, smearing the dust that had settled on my body from the extra planks, sit-ups, and sprints I had to do in the dirt. A dull ache had begun to settle in my shoulder. It was going to be another ice-and heat-night when I got home.

Would I ever have a humiliation-free day in my life again?

Our catcher, Summer, cinched her equipment bag as I passed behind her. I could feel her eyes on me as I threw my glove into my own bag and slid in my bat. My body was already heated from practice, but my cheeks were on fire, knowing Summer heard Coach chew my butt. Again.

Summer's cleats clacked against the concrete as she stepped toward me and said in a low voice, "You're a great pitcher, Tommie. You've got this."

I glanced at her T-shirt and nodded. She was wrong. If I had it together, I wouldn't have just spent the last quarter of practice in purgatory. Playoffs were around the corner. I tried to focus, get my pitches under control, be consistent, but I failed. It had been tough since prom. And some of these girls wouldn't let me live that night down.

After she left the dugout, I slipped the strap of my bag over my non-pitching shoulder and trekked through the thick air. Did everyone hear Coach yelling at me? At least I didn't cry.

I spotted Cayla, my best friend, kicked back against the spare tire of her Jeep, waiting for me. She stared down at her phone while her thumbs flew over the screen, typing. The gravel of the parking lot crunched under my shoes. She glanced up and let out a yawn.

"Up too late last night?" I asked as I approached.

Cayla gave me a look. "You know I'm not a morning person."

Most of the team hated morning practice. They were not as alert, which meant the trash talk about my prom incident was less likely to be brought up. That's why it had become my favorite time to practice.

I tried to smile, but I couldn't make it happen.

"So Coach tore you a new one?" she asked.

I reached down to untie my cleats, slipped them off, and shoved them in my bag before tossing it in the back of the vehicle. "Yeah. Did you hear?"

She shook her head. "Only the beginning." We traveled to opposite sides, climbing in. She turned the key and eased us forward through the lot. Besides the coaches, we were the last ones to leave.

"Anyone else hear?" I draped my arm along the edge of the open window. The breeze blowing in cooled my cheeks.

She shook her head and said, "I think everyone was ready to get out of here before they got called out. It was a rough practice for everyone."

I sank into my seat and closed my eyes for a minute. "Not exactly what I hoped senior year would be like." One day I would get past all the drama. I hoped it would be sooner rather than later.

"I think you pitched the best you have since... you know." She gave me a long look before turning out of the lot.

"Since prom. You can say it." On the other hand, maybe I should reconsider living at home and going to community college. *If I go to a bigger school, no one will even know who I am.* No one would remember my compromised lips plastered on the big screen.

"You said it. Does that mean you're ready to move past it?" she asked.

"Exactly." I let my head fall back against the head-rest. "I've wanted to move past it since it happened. But the video keeps showing up and the team won't let me forget."

"It's not 'the team.' Only a few. I haven't given you a hard time. Neither has Jenna nor Summer."

Strands of Cayla's russet brown hair whipped around her face from her ponytail. I reached over and nudged her shoulder, giving her a grateful smile. "I know." I was thankful for their friendship.

She grinned and turned onto my street. "I have a great idea. Let's drive over to Roan's tournament today."

I tilted my head and stared at her. Roan and I had been best buddies since he moved in the big house on the cul-de-sac of my street ten years ago. He knew everything about me, including why I hadn't been to his games lately.

She glanced over and asked, "What? You haven't watched him play in two weeks. Who will tell him what he's doing wrong if you're not there?"

"Don't you have to work for your dad?" I asked.

She shook her head. "Not if I go to the game. Please."

"First of all," I said. "I can barely face people at

school, let alone James and the rest of the baseball team. Second of all, Roan has two coaches who are more than capable of telling him what he's doing wrong."

She snickered. "Yeah, but you do it so well. And he asked if you were coming today."

"He totally understands why I'm not coming," I said. Even if he told me I was being a baby, and I needed to quit hiding.

"Come on. Face your fears." Cayla slowed, turning into my driveway to park. "I don't like going without you."

I took in a deep breath and blew it out through my teeth in a whoosh. "I know, I know. Maybe next week, okay?"

"Promise?" she asked and gripped the steering wheel as she waited for my answer.

I held back a sigh. If I promised, it would just be a lie. I opened the door. A hint of gardenias hung in the air. I breathed them in and gave her the answer she didn't want to hear. "I'll try." My feet hit the concrete and heat soaked through my socks. I caught her giant eye roll when I shut the door.

Cayla may have been shy, but she didn't have a problem with guys wanting to be more than a friend. I circled around the back. Prom ruined any chance of a boy ever asking me out. I reached in for my bag and lugged it over the edge. My shoulder was getting stiff. "What time do you have to be at the store?" I asked, stopping at the driver's door. "I'll come see you."

She held her hands up and said, "There's no way I'm going to work if I can keep from it. Dad's been in a bad mood this week. I might check with Summer or some of the other girls and see if they want to go."

I didn't blame her for wanting to go with someone else. Pre-prom, it would have been the two of us taking a road trip to the tournament. "You could hang out here. Sneak into Roan's pool with me."

"Dad would find out. He knows everyone." She rolled her eyes. "So what's for supper tonight?" she asked.

My sister and I took turns making supper. Sometimes my brother helped out. Mom usually cooked on Wednesdays. With her ever-changing schedule at the hospital, we did what we had to do. Dad's career in the Marines kept him away from his family most of the time. So he wasn't much help around the house.

I grinned and teased, "We're having protein, baby."

Cayla's dad fixed a lot of pasta. He liked meat but wasn't a good cook. "If I can't find anyone to go with, I might come over." She backed onto the street.

When I raised my arm to wave, a tinge of pain spidered through my shoulder. Ugh. I lumbered toward the house. Ice for fifteen and then a hot shower and ice again. That was the plan.

As soon as I walked inside the house, the smell of bacon enveloped me. I headed straight to the kitchen, on the verge of drooling like my little black Pug, Juju, when I spotted my sister through the wall of two-by-fours stripped of its plywood. She moved crispy bacon from the baking sheet to a plate covered with paper towels.

My stomach rumbled. "That smells amazing." I walked into the room and reached for a few pieces, but she smacked my hand. "Hey!"

Madi slid the plate out of my reach.

Poor Juju lay at Madi's feet, waiting, begging for a piece of bacon too. I leaned down and scratched behind her ear. "Juju, Sissy won't let you have any either?"

"Take me to the baseball game today and you can have some," Madi said.

I let out a growl. She should know better than to mess with me when I was hungry. "I'm not going. Give me some bacon."

"Ugh," she groaned. Her eyebrows pulled together. "Are you serious? Because of prom?"

I opened the garage door and hung my bag up. "Duh." I closed the door and washed my hands before getting the ice pack out of the freezer.

"You're being ridiculous. Nobody even talks about it anymore." The skillet sizzled after Madi cracked two eggs and dropped them in.

I nestled the ice on my shoulder. "Will you make me scrambled eggs? Please?"

She sighed but cracked two eggs in a bowl and mixed them with a fork.

I took a seat on the bar stool. "Why do you want to go to the game? You don't even like baseball."

She shuffled to the bar, biting her lip. Our lips might be about the only thing that was the same on us. I had limp, dirty blonde hair. She has thick, beautiful golden hair. She was only a freshman and already started varsity volleyball. I started varsity softball my sophomore year. She made straight A's, and I was lucky to have B average. She had bigger boobs than me and a curvier body. I was strong, lean, but straight. Except my thighs, because I did a lot of squats for power in my pitch delivery. How many girls loved having big thighs?

I'd say I was probably a three-and-a-half on a ten-point scale. She was a nine. Only because I didn't believe perfect exists.

It might be possible I harbored a tiny bit of jealousy of my sister. She had gone through two boyfriends already. I hadn't even had one and it was my senior year.

"There might be someone on the team that asked me to come to the game."

My mind raced through the team to think who it might be. "It's not James, is it?" *Please say no.* My stomach clenched, waiting for her to answer.

She stepped back to the stove. "Heck no. He may be bona fide hot, but after what happened with you?" She glanced over her shoulder at me. "Give me some credit. Geesh."

I let out my breath. Thank God. James and I had one night of history. One I wished I could forget. "Who?"

"It's…no, I don't want to jinx it," she rushed out. "Get some plates."

I stepped to the cabinet, pulled two paper plates out, and slid them across the counter to her. If she wanted to keep it a secret, fine. For the time being anyway. I fished out two forks from the silverware drawer, glasses from the cabinet to fill with milk, and sat down.

Madi plated our food and sat beside me. "What about Roan? You know he wants you to be there."

Guilt from telling my two best friends no grew heavy on my chest. I knew Roan liked me to be at his games, but he also knew why I couldn't. "Cayla was looking for someone to go with her," I said and took a big drink.

Madi tucked a piece of her nearly perfect bed-head hair behind her ear and asked, "Do you think she'd mind me going with her?"

I shook my head, pulling my phone out of my pocket to send Cayla a message.

Tommie: You still looking for someone to go to the games?

Cayla: You're going???? Say yes!

Tommie: Madi wants to go.

Cayla: How about you?

Tommie: Nope. Just Madi.

Cayla: Tell her I'll pick her up in 45 minutes.

I showed Madi the message.

"Crap. Guess I better eat fast. I still need to take a shower." Madi took a bite of her eggs. "Come with us."

Juju put her paws on my feet and whined. I snickered and slipped her a piece of my bacon. "If everyone will be at the game, maybe I could get some beach time in."

"You can't stay home for the rest of your life. You're already going stir-crazy." She downed her drink and shoveled the last bit of food from her plate into her mouth. "I cooked. You clean." She smirked and ran out of the kitchen.

I TURNED MY LAMP OFF AND HUNKERED underneath my blankets. Madi and Cayla hadn't made it back from their road trip to the baseball tournament. That meant I didn't have to fix supper tonight since Brendan said he was going out. That happened often since he graduated last year.

Mom came home a half-hour ago and went straight to her bedroom. Everyone was busy.

I stroked Juju's coat. "It's just me and you against the world, girl." A heaviness pushed down on my chest, so I rolled to my side. It showed up a lot since prom. It usually only appeared when I was alone now.

I scrolled through social media for any new comments about my transformation into a guppy or kissing James or any of the myriad of hurtful headlines people came up with. Nothing new. That I saw anyway.

When I looked up James, the stupid video was at the top of his list. Still.

Every time I saw it on a post, I relived the moment. Not that I wanted to.

James led me through the crowd to the middle of the dance floor, surrounded by couples. Halfway through the song, he found the edge of the ribbons that crisscrossed along my exposed spine. His fingers danced on my bare back, and he asked me to skip post prom and go to the beach. I was so excited to be at prom with him, I would have gone anywhere he wanted. Especially since he was so dreamy all night. He was more of a jock than me. And good-looking. And did I mention dreamy?

The thought of leaving made me nervous though, because he had a tiny reputation for kissing a lot of girls. But that's what I wanted, right? Someone who knew what they were doing. The song was ending, and the DJ said something about memories.

Camera flashes popped around us, but James kept his eyes and hands on me.

I knew if I left and Mom found out, I would be so grounded. But *James Lowe* asked, and the way he looked at me...

It took like two seconds for me to say yes. James pulled me against his body. I knew, at that moment, he was going to kiss me. My first kiss. I watched him close his eyes and lean his mouth toward mine. I didn't want to miss a single millisecond of what was happening. My heart slammed against my rib cage I was so nervous and excited.

His hands made a wrong turn, slid down to my backside, and he squeezed his hands full of my tush! I gasped. My mouth popped open in surprise just as our lips should have touched.

I FISH-LIPPED HIM!

We jerked apart. The look of disgust on his face was a line drive to the gut. Laughter erupted from all around us as people pointed toward the DJ.

I looked in that direction. The camera person making "memories" caught my first kiss debacle on live video. My humiliation played on a fast loop. I was mortified.

I fled the dance floor to the bathroom and hid in a stall, crying my eyes out. There was no way I could go back out there with my giant fish lips blown up on that screen.

Cayla and Roan found me. It was so sweet that he barreled into the girl's restroom and shooed everyone out. Cayla stayed with her date, but Roan snuck me out of the building and drove me home.

He had since tried to get James to take the video off his post, but James wouldn't do it.

I needed the courage to ask James myself.

Juju whined.

"I know, girl. I haven't been able to face him."

Guys made kissing noises or sucked their cheeks together until their mouth formed fish lips as they passed by in the halls at school. Of course, they only did it when Roan wasn't with me.

My phone buzzed with a message from Cayla.

Cayla: Want ice cream?
Tommie: No thanks. Going to sleep.

I wasn't really tired, but I didn't want Madi coming into my room and bragging about how much fun she had. The baseball guys used to be my territory. I had my eyes set on a couple of them when school started. That was my hope. But it never happened. Until the debacle with James.

Another message came across.

Roan: Won one. Lost one.

Tommie: Sorry. How did you play?

Roan: Not great. Stopping at the Burger Bar with the team. Cayla and Madi will be there.

Tommie: I'm sure you were fine. Have fun.

It was Saturday night, I was eighteen, and I was at home in bed. If I stayed in Sweet Water, North Carolina, the rest of my life, I'll die without ever being kissed again.

2

P astor Bryant spoke from the short platform at the front of the church building. I tried to listen, but I wasn't able to focus. His son, Jett, had his arm around his girlfriend in the second pew. Jett was so nice and tall and good-looking.

Across the aisle from him, Charlotte and Lucas were just as cozy. Lucas was gorgeous and treated her like a queen. Their cuteness had my heart in a free-fall, and I had to close my eyes so I'd stop feeling sorry for myself.

Roan bumped my shoulder and whispered, "Wake up."

We didn't always sit together. His grandparents liked to sit in different spots and he usually sat with them.

I wanted to pull my phone out and see how much longer I had to endure watching these couples, but Mom would confiscate it for a week.

I leaned close to Roan and asked, "Have you noticed how many couples are in this church? It's depressing."

He glanced around. His eyebrows rose as he asked, "You're jealous?"

I shrugged and then nodded.

The corner of his mouth lifted. He slid his arm behind me, resting it on the back of the pew. "Is that better?"

I narrowed my eyes, pouting my lips, and huffed, "Not quite the same." I didn't ask him to move it though.

Mom nudged me and gave me the look that said I better stop talking or else.

As soon as the service was over, Roan and I weaved in and out of the crowd to get out of there. If I had to watch the lovebirds holding hands one more second, my heart would turn into stone. And the way the day was going, James would show up any second to shatter it .

When I hit the fresh air, I was able to breathe.

"Want a ride?" Roan asked, navigating us down the steps toward the parking lot.

"Yes. Get me out of here. I need to send Mom a quick message." I typed the passcode into my phone.

"Already told her we were leaving." He unlocked his Toyota truck, and we split apart to climb in.

"You know me so well." And he did know me. For half of my life, we had been best friends.

As soon as we were both in, Roan brought the engine to life and took off.

"I think I was getting claustrophobic." At least that was the excuse I gave Roan.

He scoffed. "Is that what you call it?"

I let out a groan. "I can't help that I'm not Roan Martin, baseball beast and heartbreaker."

"Whatever," he mumbled and turned into our subdivision.

I shook my head. "Don't 'whatever' me. You're getting a scholarship to Tennessee. That says you're a beast. And you have a ton of girls who would go out with you, but you're too good for them. Which," I poked his shoulder, "I don't mind because then we'd never get to hang out."

He made another turn and drove down our street. "Hey, that goes both ways, you know." He grinned, glancing in my direction.

Roan had a way about him that always kept me from falling apart. He didn't allow just anyone to see that side of him. Or maybe it was that I knew him for so long and ignored the grizzly bear act.

We came to a stop in front of my house. "We're supposed to drive to Myrtle Beach to meet some old client of Gramp's today. I'd rather stay home, but that wasn't an option."

I smiled and hitched my shoulder. "Guess I'll swim

without you."

"Where were you Saturday?" he asked.

Guilt put a knot in my stomach. I tilted my head. "Roan..."

His grandparents drove past and honked.

I changed the subject and said, "I don't know why you have to drive separately."

He shrugged. "I like to drive. Gramps likes to drive. You're coming to the game tomorrow, right?"

The knots in my belly twisted like a pretzel. I tried to worm my way out of going. "I don't know. I have practice."

He looked out his windshield. The teasing smile he'd been wearing was gone. "I gotta go."

"Okay." His grandparents had turned the vehicle around and were waiting for him. I opened the door and hopped down to the pavement. "Have fun."

"Yeah." He didn't sound thrilled. I don't know if it was because he didn't want to drive to Myrtle Beach or that he knew I wasn't going to his game.

I shut the door and crossed behind his truck as he took off. Pre-prom, I wouldn't have missed a game or even a practice of his if I didn't have my own going on. Cayla was right. I coached Roan, and he coached me. That's the way it had always been.

But that was before my first kiss turned into a nightmare.

3

I opened the back of Cayla's Jeep, tossed my stuff in, and closed the door. She said Brendan helped her put the rag top on before she drove to the baseball game Saturday. Which was odd because I thought he was working.

When I climbed in the front, Madi's voice shot out from the back seat, "You got your butt chewed again?"

I jumped. My hand flew to my chest. "Oh, my gosh!" I took a few breaths. "A warning would have been nice."

"I thought you heard us talking when you put your stuff in the back," Cayla said with a giggle.

"I had other things on my mind." I twisted to look at Madi. "What are you doing here?"

She gave me a sheepish grin and shrugged. "I had a volleyball meeting after school. Cayla said she'd give me a ride home."

Cayla gave my sister rides? This was new. I raised my eyebrows at my best friend and silently asked what was going on.

"What did Coach say?" Cayla asked, ignoring my look and starting the engine.

I tossed a hand up in the air. "Mazzie's starting."

"What?" Cayla and Madi responded at the same time.

"I suck, I guess." I knew I needed to snap out of my funk, but it was easier said than done.

Cayla pulled out of the parking lot.

"You don't suck," Madi said, leaning forward between the seats.

Cayla turned out of the parking lot in the opposite direction of my house.

"Where are you going?" I asked. "My house is this way." I pointed with my thumb behind us.

"Well," she sang, dragging the word out, making it two syllables. "Madi and I want to watch the rest of the baseball game."

"What? No. I'm not going." I swiveled in my seat and glared at my sister. "Is this your idea? You're only a freshman, you know. And Cayla's not your personal driver."

Cayla patted my arm. "Calm down. It was my idea."

The pounding in my head from Coach's booming voice and demotion doubled down in my skull. I pulled the hairband out of my ponytail and tried to ease the pain by massaging my scalp. "My day has been bad enough. I can't take another punch to my pride."

"Baby steps," Cayla said, smiling as if she was doing me a favor. She turned down the path for baseball parking.

Most people sat in the stands or in foldable chairs they brought with them. Only a few people stayed in their cars, parked along the first and third base fences. My jaw was set tight. "I'm not getting out," I said.

"That's okay." Cayla said, driving down the third base path. "We can see Roan catch on this side." She maneuvered the Jeep in an open spot with a view of home plate. Unfortunately, it had a prime location to see directly into the home dugout too. Ugh.

The scoreboard showed the game was at the bottom of the eighth inning, and the Lions were up 3 to 2 over the Panthers. One on first base and one out.

"Watch the runner on first," I said. "I'm calling it. He's going to try to steal second."

Madi and Cayla chattered about me getting out of the house, but I tuned them out. My eyes roamed back and forth between Roan and the runner. I knew the runner was going for it. I had that gut feeling.

"That's it!" Cayla yelled, startling me and turning my attention away from the game.

I glanced at her for only a second, and just as I was turning back to the runner, Cayla clasped my face in her hands. Her eyes wide and excited, she burst out, "A kissing tutor!"

My eyebrows knit together. I didn't know what she was talking about, but I had a feeling the runner was going to steal. I twisted out of her grip and focused back on the game. The player slid into second base as the ball hit the dirt in front of it. "What? No!" I called out.

The outfield umpire's arms flew straight out to his sides. The runner was safe.

My gaze made a beeline for Roan. He sat back on his heels, hand and glove perched on his thighs, and knees in the dirt. Judging by the jerky movement of his head, he used a few choice words to chew himself out.

Madi made a hissing noise. "Ooo, that's not good."

I leaned out the window and yelled, "Shake it off, Catch!"

Roan's head popped up. He called a time, got off his knees, and stalked toward the pitcher's mound, searching in my direction. He pulled his mask up and gazed at me.

I cupped my hands around my mouth and yelled, "You've got this, Martin!"

He touched his glove to the top of his head, then to his chest, and tapped his leg twice with it. That was our sign that said, "I hear you."

I slid back through the window and growled at Madi, "What's the deal with you and baseball all of a sudden?"

"I told you," she said. Her voice was full of tenacity. "I was invited."

I rolled my eyes. I would find out, eventually.

"Did you hear me?" Madi asked. It wasn't a question she intended me to answer because she continued without pause, "Cayla and I have a good idea."

"Good?" Cayla raised her hands in the air. "It's brilliant!"

While Cayla took a breath before spilling whatever was on her mind, I watched Roan march back to the plate as I took my cleats and socks off. Yuck, I hated sweaty feet. At least they didn't stink.

"Tommie, my friend, we've solved your problems."

I scoffed. "Oh, yeah?" The crack of a bat cut through the buzz of their chatter. The batter hit a pop fly. James ran underneath it and caught it for an out. It had been two weeks since I watched Roan and the baseball team play. I missed it.

The continued clap of Madi's hands made it clear she was excited about their solution. I already had my doubts. If my sister was involved, it would be a plan where she would end up winning.

"You remember when I was having trouble with chemistry last year?" Cayla asked.

I nodded.

She tilted her head down with her dark eyebrows arched. Cayla had nicely shaped, well-manicured eyebrows that were a bit darker than her russet hair. Which was equally as nice, but it was pulled back into a ponytail at the moment. She continued, "And what did I do to catch up?"

The crowd cheered, and I glanced up to see our team jogging to the dugout. The scoreboard showed no change in runs. The Lions were up to bat. Would Roan bat this inning?

"Uh," I mumbled, turning back to the girls. "You got someone smarter to teach you. Who was it, that science nerd who sits in the middle of our English class? Roy something."

Madi snickered, but Cayla sighed. "Rudy. Rudy Lopez. The guy's name is not the point. The point *is* I found someone who knew what they were doing and asked for help."

"And?" I tilted my head back and forth, waiting for her to spell it out for me before the first Lion's batter stepped into the box.

She let out a growl.

"Come on, Tommie. You're not that dense." Madi smacked my knee and leaned back in her seat, folding her arms against her chest.

I giggled. Not that I was trying, but aggravating my sister was a bonus. "Sorry. Between the game and your riddles, I'm not following."

The clink of a baseball making contact with an

aluminum bat rang out. I scanned the ball diamond to see Logan Scott running to first base and then to second. Nice start to the ninth inning for our Lions.

"Tommie Sue Jenkins," Cayla said, using her stern, I-mean-business voice.

I turned and gave her my full attention, wearing a smirk. "Yes, Cayla Louise Masterson?"

Cayla let out a frustrated growl. "We're trying to help you here."

"Yeah, Tommie," Madi added.

"Okay, okay. I'm focused." I leaned toward her, giving her my full attention.

That seemed to satisfy her. A grin spread across her lips that meant Cayla had either a devilish or brilliant plan. Possibly both. She announced, "In order to boost your reputation and move past your very public, humiliating first kiss...you need to secure a hot kissing tutor."

My mouth fell open. Heat spread from my ears to my cheeks. "A kissing tutor? You want me to ask someone to teach me how to kiss?"

"Not just *a* kissing tutor. A *hot* kissing tutor." Madi said it as if "hot" made the difference in the whole idea that I even needed one in the first place.

"As if a video of me, swallowing James' lips like a giant goldfish, playing on repeat at prom wasn't humiliating enough? How do you think asking someone to teach me how to kiss will feel?" I covered my face with my hands. Had it come to this? "As if that would ever work out in a positive way."

Cayla peeled my hands away. "Name the top five hottest guys." She held a finger up, waiting for the first one.

I could think of plenty of hot guys. In fact, I had them doodled in a notebook I had hidden in my shorts drawer. Even though I was sure they had both lost their minds, I knew they wouldn't let up until I gave them something. "I can name more than that. James Lowe, Jason Hunt, Jett Bryant, Logan Scott, Jeremiah Dermot, Lucas Addington, Brantley Nelson, Carson Brooks, Ky Andrews, Wes Shultz, Parker Lewis, Gabe Washington."

Madi jumped in. "Except for James, they're all taken, dork. You can't use any of them."

I shrugged. "You didn't specify they needed to be single. Guess there's no more humiliation in my future."

"It doesn't have to be like that." Cayla shifted in her seat. "You're a pretty girl. What guy wouldn't want to have a few no-strings-attached make-out sessions?"

Madi bumped her fist to Cayla's. "This is so brilliant."

If there were any boys who agreed with Cayla, I wouldn't have had to talk Roan into helping me find a prom date. I swiveled in my seat, turning back to the game. "Brilliantly demoralizing." I groaned. Roan stepped from the on-deck circle to the batter's box.

Cayla continued her sales pitch. The more she talked, the more my resolve against the idea waned. I considered if I had the guts to ask a boy to be my kissing tutor. How many more blows could my pride and confidence take before they shattered?

I glanced to the field and watched Roan dig in to the batter's box. Roan watched the first pitch float by. It was outside—ball one. The pitcher checked the runners on first and third, made his windup, and delivered. The clink of Roan's hit echoed all the way to the Jeep. The ball flew to centerfield and bounced off the fence. I crawled up and sat on the frame of the door window, whooping and cheering for Roan.

Since it hit the fence, it was considered a double. But two runners where able to make it home. That meant we were up 5 to 2. I watched him settle on second base. His grin was missing though.

"What about Roan?" Cayla asked.

I stiffened for a few seconds, wondering what she meant. Was Roan hot? Duh. That didn't mean he needed to know I thought that. Besides Cayla, Roan was my best friend. We practically grew up together.

I slid back inside and folded one leg on the seat. "What about him?" I asked Cayla, as if I wasn't just thinking about how good-looking I thought Roan was.

"Maybe he can hook you up with one of the baseball guys," she said.

It took a lot of begging to get him to help me with my prom date. "I don't know. He did me a favor with James. Look how great that turned out."

Madi gasped. "What about Max Yeager?"

"No." I shook my head. "What is he, like twelve?"

"He's a sophomore, but look at him." Madi pointed toward the stands.

"He probably knows as much about kissing as I do." I cocked my head to the side, considering it anyway, and scanned the area for a more likely candidate. Tucked around the corner of the stands was Jerrick Locke, tall, dark, and handsome in every way. He had a bad boy vibe. Coach Crawford kicked him off the baseball team last year. "Maybe I need to be thinking more along the bad boy path. Do you see Jerrick?"

"Mm-hmm," Cayla hummed. "Bad boys do have more experience."

I stared across the field at Max and Jerrick. "Okay, I might be able to get behind this idea."

Cayla snickered. "We need a few options. Who else do we put on the list?"

4

The sliding glass door of Roan's house opened and closed. I looked up from the float I was lying on in the pool and saw him hobble to the hot tub and slide the top off.

The movement drew my eyes to his abs as they flexed. I moved my gaze to his cloudy golden eyes. "You weren't kidding when you said it was a rough game, huh?" I asked, keeping my eyes on his face while I paddled toward the edge of the pool. Well... I tried not to look at his bare torso, but he was more defined than most baseball players on his team.

Roan winced, lifting his leg over the side, and it made his pecs dance.

I forced myself to look away. It was all Cayla and Madi's fault. All that talk about hot guys had messed with my head.

"Nope," he answered.

I looked back at him as his other foot plunked into the water. He sank into the steam until his wide shoulders were immersed. "Why didn't you come with Cayla and Madi Saturday?"

I thought he dropped this yesterday. He knew why I didn't go. Everyone in the universe knew why I didn't go. I ignored his question and asked my own. "How'd you let that guy steal on you in the eighth inning?"

He lifted his hand out of the water, held up three fingers, and grumbled, "Three times. And I don't know. If I keep this up, they may not want me at Tennessee." Roan rested his head back on the ledge and closed his lids. Tennessee offered him a scholarship, as did several other colleges, but his grandparents said he couldn't commit until the end of school.

I scaled the side of the pool and dripped all the way to the hot tub. Roan and his grandparents didn't seem to mind that I made myself at home in their pool whenever I wanted. When he texted me after the game to come over, I was happy to do so. Plus, it gave me the opportunity to ask for his help.

"What did Coach Rojas have to say?" I skipped the steps, hopped up on the edge of the tub, and spun around.

Roan's eyes popped open as I dipped my toes in. He watched my body slide under the water and said, "The usual. Get your head in the game. React faster. Watch my signs." He mimicked coach's drill sergeant voice. "I don't know what the deal is. I played better after I heard you though." A small smile played on his lips. "I think you're my good-luck charm."

I gave him a genuine toothy grin, shaking his leg with my foot. "Aw, I've never been a good-luck charm before."

He ignored my sweetness. "My stance must be off or something because my knees are killing me."

Being off...that I could definitely associate with. "Yeah, Coach has been on my case too."

"Pitch and catch in the morning." He said it like an order, but that was just Roan. His eyebrows hung over his deep-set eyes in a glower.

Being six feet-tall with thick shoulders made him seem intimidating to most people. To me? Not so much. Although, I had to say, when he bored his liquid caramel eyes on me, fog had a tendency to fill my head.

I played copy-cat, mimicking his every expression, until he chuckled and told me to stop it. Making him smile seemed to excite my insides. I liked that feeling. Besides, he was too handsome to allow him to keep a scowl on his face.

He raised his legs one at a time, resting his feet on top of my knees. "Your coach is right. You haven't been focused."

I shrugged. "I'll check out your position in the morning. You can tell me what I'm doing wrong then." I reached a hand to my upper arm and kneaded around my pitching shoulder. "I've iced my shoulder after every practice this week. And Coach isn't starting me tomorrow even when it's my rotation."

"That sucks." He motioned with his hand for me to sit next to him. "Let me feel your shoulder."

Roan was a little on the brawny side, including his hands. When it came to a pulled or strained muscle, or pain in my shoulder though, he had a magic touch. I crossed through the warm water and sat next to him, angling away so he could inspect my pitching arm.

His fingertips touched my skin and, as it had since last summer, tingles radiated in every direction from his contact.

Roan continued his inspection. "There's no swelling. That's good. Keep icing it."

I nodded.

He raised my elbow and rotated my arm in a big circle. "Any pain?"

"Nope. Just a sore, dull ache. Like I can feel my pulse in it." I craned my neck to look back at him.

He released my arm and slid to the corner, tapping the button for the jets. "I'll check it in the morning before we warm up."

"Thanks." I slid over to another corner. The jets were more powerful in the corner than the sides.

The conversation with Cayla and Madi filled my head. With playoffs and graduation only weeks away, I didn't have the luxury of time. It was now or never. Did I really want to be known in this town for the rest of my life for sucking James' lips? Heck no!

Roan had been there for all my dumb ideas and silly pranks. He'd been there every time Dad left and when I locked myself in the bathroom at prom. He had seen it all. "Roan?"

"Hm?" he hummed.

I glanced over to see his closed eyelids. One thing about Roan having a dark complexion and dark hair was being able to see his eyelashes. Mine were light like my hair. If I didn't wear mascara, they seemed sparse and short. Almost nonexistent.

"Cayla and Madi came up with an idea." My stomach clenched. I knew my request would sound crazy, but I didn't have any other options to fix my reputation.

"What, hi-jack my pool?" He leaned over the side of the tub for his phone, which was laying on the table, and checked the time.

"Um, no." Not that Cayla and me lying around poolside would be unusual. I let Madi come sometimes. It's not like we didn't have a beach within walking distance.

"We've been in here long enough," he said, laying his phone back on the table.

We both climbed out and jumped into the cool water of the pool. My body stiffened at the difference in temperature. He swam the length of it, and I met him at the shallow end.

"I need your help with something. It's embarrassing, but it's the only way we can think of so I don't go down as the worst kisser of Sweet Water High."

He chuckled, shaking his head. "Oh, this ought to be good."

I swallowed and turned toward the wall of the pool. "I need a tutor." Ugh, admitting it out loud was more difficult than I thought it would be.

"For what, pre-calc?"

Pre-calc wasn't my favorite subject, but I did okay in it. I acted like I was stretching my arm, hoping to tamp down the uptick in my heart rate. "I need a kissing tutor."

His whole face pinched together.

"Do you think Max Yeager would be good? Or maybe I should go a different route with Jerrick Locke?"

Roan stared at me as if I had grown two long ears, a long snout, and buck teeth.

A growly whine came out of me. "Quit looking at me like a jackass."

He scoffed. "Quit acting like one."

I clamped my hands on my hips and asked, "Do you have a better idea?"

"Toms," he said in a masculine whine. His posture softened as he rested his elbows on the ledge behind him. Roan was the only person who called me Toms. It was short for Tommie Sue.

"I can't be that person who comes back to their high school reunion and have no one remember what a great pitcher I was or how nice and friendly and outgoing I was all four years. They'll only remember one thing."

He stared off across the pool with his stupid, bored look, the one he wore when he didn't like my comment. He didn't utter a word.

My knees held my weight against the floor of the pool even though I wanted to sink under the water and hide my embarrassment. Instead, I folded my arms on the ledge and rested my chin on top of them. Tears pricked my eyes, and I didn't want him to see them. "It's not only that. I think I really need help. It was—" I sighed—"Is, obvious I don't know what I'm doing when it comes to kissing. It doesn't help my cause that boys just don't seem to like me that way. It's like I have an invisible sign that reads, ONE OF THE GUYS."

"Sounds like drama to me." He shook his head and said, "Guys don't worry about that crap. You just need to man up and get back in the game." He shrugged as if it was no big deal. It was like the hundredth time he'd said it was no big deal.

A rogue tear spilled over my eyelid. I quickly wiped it away. "You know what?" I stood and stepped in front of him. "I'm not a guy." I swung my arms out and spun around. "See? I have boobs and everything."

"Cut it out. That's not what I meant." He grasped for my wrist, but I tugged it out of his reach.

My eyes burned with tears as they trickled out one right after another in a steady stream. I had to get out of there before he told me guys don't cry. I waded to the ladder, climbed out of the pool, and snatched my towel off of the chair.

"Where are you going?" he asked.

"See you in the morning," I snapped. At least I tried to be as snippy and snotty as possible, but I think I came across exactly what I was.

Pathetic.

I PLANTED MY BUTT IN THE SAND AND LEANED MY back against the Surf Shack on the beach. My brother managed the business since last summer after graduating. He closed it up about an hour ago. With the overhanging ledge, it was the perfect place to watch the tide roll in without people noticing me.

After leaving Roan's house in tears, I knew I needed endorphins to get me out of the funk. Usually I'd do something fun like a cannon ball contest with Roan or go work out. Doing anything with him was out of the question, and I didn't want to risk putting too much strain on my shoulder with weights. I planned to jog to the section where bonfires and cars were allowed. But when I got here, Logan, Esme, James, and another girl were playing around by the water, walking and flirting in the direction I was headed.

Tommie Jenkins is a fun, upbeat person. At least I used to be. I wanted to be that person again, but I couldn't seem to shake the flashing sign over my head that said, OPEN SEASON FOR LAUGHS.

Sand flew across my toes. I glanced up and saw Roan and then focused back on the horizon.

He sat beside me. Not that I wanted him to.

It was high tide, and I liked the way the waves roared onto the beach. The noise level ticked up a notch and helped drown out the drama in my head.

I finally asked, "What are you doing here?"

"I was thinking, you should try to make the University of Tennessee's softball team. My contact there said they usually hold back a scholarship for last minute. He thought their softball coaches did that too."

I pulled my knees closer to my chest. It wasn't a terrible idea. I planned on living at home for the next two years, but running away from Sweet Water and bad memories of my senior year was tempting.

Roan's hand brushed my ponytail before he twirled it around his fingers. "I know you wanted to live at home and go to Sweet Water College, but it would be fun for us to go to Tennessee together. Don't you think?"

The bad mood Roan put me in took a hit from his sweetness sledgehammer. It wasn't possible, but the thought made me feel better. A corner of my mouth lifted. "It would be fun, but I can't even start on my high school team. There's no way I could make the team, let alone snag a scholarship to Tennessee."

"Your coach is just trying to motivate you." His fingers released my hair and slid over to my shoulder, pulling me against his strong frame. "Y'all have a chance to go to state and she needs you to focus. Whether or not you believe it, you are a team leader."

Things had shifted the last couple of weeks. I wasn't a leader. Not anymore. Backstabbing and gossip had taken my place. It didn't seem like the baseball team ever had to deal with stuff like that.

"What was that?" Roan asked with a playful tone. "I'm always right? You've finally acknowledged my brilliance?"

I chuckled and tossed a jab at his abs. Not one word about him being right had slipped across my lips. He was teasing.

He clutched at his shirt and acted like I caught him

off guard, but it was my go-to when he teased me like this.

"Tommie, girl," he growled, pulling me on top of him and then flipping us over with my back pressed into the sand. "I can't let you get away with that." He grinned, and the way his eyes smoldered stopped my breathing for a second or five. He had the most beautiful caramel-colored eyes I'd ever seen.

He dipped his mouth next to my ear and whispered, "Two words...tickle monster."

I gasped for breath and shrieked, "No!"

Just as the word left my mouth, his fingers dug into my sides, causing uncontrollable giggles to pour out of me. I squirmed underneath him and tried to push his hands away, but any progress I made was short-lived.

"Who's brilliant?" he asked, offering me a way to stop his tickling.

I shook my head and managed to squeak out, "Me."

His eyes widened with his smile. "Wrong answer." He reached one hand back and squeezed right above my knee.

My legs flailed and kicked, but he was better at this game.

"Toms," he sang, "who's brilliant?"

If I could have breathed a little better, I would've held out, but I had to give up. "Roan," I squeaked out and took a breath. "Roan Martin."

He stopped tickling but held me in place. We both laughed, and he was breathing as heavily as I was.

He did that thing with his eyes again, leaning nose to nose. "Don't you forget it."

It caused my belly to dip, but I laughed right in his face so he didn't notice what he'd done.

He shook his head, wearing a smile, and stood, pulling me up with him. "Now I have sand in my shoes."

"Good," I shot back, still full of laughter. The way we acted sometimes was juvenile. But when you grow up together, it's easy to revert to the silly kid stuff.

He looped his arm around the back of my neck and put us in motion toward the road where his truck was parked. "Let's go get some chili cheese fries at the Burger Bar."

I hitched a shoulder. "Okay." The good thing about getting food there was I didn't have to get out of the truck.

"And then we'll go back to your house and you can check out Tennessee's softball team."

The thought of being out on my own, away from my family scared the crap out of me. Although I didn't think I would miss my little sister much. It wouldn't be so bad if I knew what I wanted to do with my future. "Roan," I said in a half-sigh, half-whine.

"Toms," he mimicked my voice. "I'm serious. It

wouldn't be a bad thing for us to go to the same college. Get away from here."

Going to school away from home wasn't a terrible idea. I could leave the prom drama behind that way. If I had a good friend going too, all the better. But leaving Mom or Juju? And what if Dad got leave, came home, and I didn't get to see him? "I'll think about it."

Roan and I came to school early for pitch and catch. He pointed out my stride was off and caused my arm to overexert. I noticed his footing was too narrow and he didn't have his toes pointed outward. We were good like this.

He didn't mention anything about helping me find a kissing tutor though. And I didn't want a repeat of yesterday, so I left it alone. He went straight to his coach's office when we walked into Sweet Water High.

Cayla stood by my locker, waiting for me. "Did you practice this morning?" she asked.

"Yeah. Just pitch and catch with Roan," I said as I flipped the combination on my lock and opened the door.

She leaned her head close to the opening and asked, "Did he say anything this morning? What exactly went down yesterday?" Cayla asked in her exasperated voice.

She used it quite often when it came to Roan. "I need to figure out if we should wait on him or not."

She sent me a message last night, wanting to know how it went. I couldn't bring myself to type the words of why I stormed off from Roan's house yesterday. Anyone could see that I wasn't the most girly-looking girl. But I lived with it every day. It wasn't necessary for Roan to point it out to me. And after he came looking for me at the beach, I didn't want to think about it anymore. So I told Cayla we'd talk this morning.

I shut the door as students surged through the hallway. Maybe I should ask her the truth. If I did look like a boy, there was no hope of finding even one person who was willing to be my kissing tutor.

We stopped at her locker. Roan's was just a couple down from hers. I glanced around. If anyone heard what I was about to say, I would never be able to come back to school. I leaned close so only she could hear me and said, "I left. I couldn't take another reference to me being a guy."

A crease formed between her eyebrows as we moved to her locker. "He said," she glanced around before mouthing the words, "you were a guy?"

"He might as well have. Tell me, honestly—pinky swear truth—do I?" I turned three-hundred-sixty degrees as I had with Roan in the pool.

"Not that again." Roan's voice hit me from behind.

I rolled my eyes and leaned against the locker next to Cayla's. Roan didn't bring up my request last night or this morning when we were practicing. He's methodical, and I was trying as hard as I could to be patient. There wasn't much school left, which meant I needed to act fast or forget the whole thing.

Roan stepped beside me, resting his forearm on my shoulder.

Cayla narrowed her eyes at him, pulling her lip up in a snarl. She moved her gaze back to me, cocking her head to the side. "No dude should have a figure like yours. You have plenty of girly attributes." She nodded to my boobs. "I wish mine were that nice."

I rolled my eyes and straightened. "Whatever."

"I'm serious." She grabbed her calculator, notebook, and pencil from her locker before closing it. Turning back to Roan, she asked, "Did you talk to Max yet?"

A long breath whistled through his nose. "Look, we have playoffs to focus on. You shouldn't be thinking about stuff like this right now." He shifted, removing his arm from my shoulder, and shoved a hand in his pocket.

Cayla's eyebrows popped high on her forehead. "You mean to tell me asking someone out, or making out, never enters your guy brain because you're focused on play-offs?" Her voice was a little loud.

Roan looked around at the hallway. A few people with quizzical expressions looked in our direction. He narrowed his eyes and took a step closer to Cayla. "Do y'all want to go to state?"

Cayla nodded in the direction behind Roan and me and mumbled, "Doesn't seem to bother some of your teammates."

I turned and saw James and one of his exes locking lips in a doorway as if it was shielding them from being seen. It took me a few seconds, maybe minutes, to look away. A groan slipped out of my mouth, and I tilted my head back to stare at the white ceiling. Why couldn't I have looked that good kissing James Lowe?

After a bit of awkward silence, Roan said, "That's just James. Besides, we've got finals coming up."

"Ha," I scoffed, leaning against the cool, green metal of the lockers. "I know for a fact that your grades were high enough to opt out of all your finals except one. So don't feed me that line."

Roan tossed a hand in the air. "I don't know what exactly you want me to do." He stepped closer. "You want me to make an announcement at practice? How much are you paying for these services?"

Cayla and I looked at each other. We didn't think about paying anyone.

The thought squeezed my heart. If my body crumpled any more, I would have been a blob on the floor "Am I so pathetic that I have to pay?"

Cayla's mouth dropped open. "Of course not." Her gaze locked on to Roan. "Right, Roan?"

He shrugged. "How am I supposed to know?"

Seriously? He's a guy. Shouldn't he know these things? Unless he did know and said that to prepare me.

Cayla's lips pressed into a thin line.

"Great," I uttered. "Just..." Frustration wound inside me like a spring. I banged the back of my head against the lockers a few times. "Awesome." The sting of tears forming hit me. I closed my eyes for a second before focusing on Roan's Puma tennis shoes. He always wore name-brand stuff—always looked nice.

I checked Cayla's wardrobe; pink Converse, cute white shorts, and pink top.

Me? School was about to begin, and I looked as if practice was about to start. My heart squeezed even tighter. Any hope this idea of Cayla and Madi's would work was eroding.

"You're so thick!" Cayla growled at Roan. "Just put some feelers out there."

"Tommie, you don't have to go along with this dumb idea," Roan grumbled.

Cayla sliced her hand through the air. "Forget about it, then. I'm sure we can do this without the help of the almighty Roan Martin." Cayla could be a beast on the softball field, but this was aggressive for her off the field. It was not her normal shy manner. "Oh, look," she sang.

"There's our first customer and number one on our list, Jerrick."

I lifted my gaze as Cayla smoothed down her shirt. "Come on, Tommie." She linked arms with me and put us in motion.

I glanced over my shoulder and said to Roan, "Maybe dumb ideas are all I have to work with."

Summer and Mazzie walked in front of me to the softball diamond. Pitchers and catchers were always first on the field to warm up before the game. It was Mazzie's day to start, and after realizing this morning I might have to pay someone to kiss me, I didn't feel much like chatting and made sure to keep to myself on the way out.

The crunch of cleats and the ear-piercing pitch of London Hauser's shrill giggle shot past me from behind like an arrow. It wasn't long before another grinding voice grated on me.

Tommy Styles, baseball jerk extraordinaire and benchwarmer, not so casually called, "Oh, look, it's the fake Tommy. Come on. Let's go say hello." He started calling me the fake Tommy because I'm a girl with a boy's name. At least he acknowledged I was a girl. That was the only good thing about the guy.

London giggled, causing me to flinch. "Hey, there, guppy girl."

Their footsteps gained on my position, picking up speed. They split on either side of me, both making kissing noises with their cheeks sucked in and their lips opening and closing like a goldfish.

My stomach clenched as I slowed my pace and put more distance between us. It wasn't the first time it had happened to me. Doubted it would be the last. But I still wanted to crawl in a hole every time.

The faint ruckus of gear rattling together grew louder as it got closer. "Get me a drink before you start warming the bench, Styles," Roan called from behind me. His heavy steps quickly approached until we were side by side. "Why do you let them do that?" He switched his bag full of catching gear to the other shoulder.

My jaw clenched before I answered, "What do you want me to do? Beat them up? That would really help people forget about it, now wouldn't it?"

He let out a long breath.

"This is why I need," I glanced around us to make sure no one was within hearing distance, "a tutor. Someone to teach me how to be great at kissing and then want to kiss me in public. Even if I have to pay for it. It will turn everything around. And," I held up my crossed fingers, "I could even get a boyfriend out of the deal."

"Who cares what people like Styles and London think? If Lowe hadn't grabbed your butt, you wouldn't have freaked out."

"It's almost the whole school, Roan. It doesn't matter why it looked like I was trying to eat his lips. A picture is worth more than a thousand words, or even the truth."

He shook his head and pushed out another long breath. "That's why you should come to Tennessee."

"It's probably too late for that."

The red and gold colors of the visiting Eagles' jerseys were sprinkled throughout the outfield. The baseball field was past the softball diamond. Their field was nicer than ours, surrounded by trees, and it had a nice scoreboard and great lights.

"Mazzie's starting today?" he asked. It was her normal rotation, but she didn't have more than three innings in her before her arm would need rest.

I nodded. "Yeah."

"If you get put in, remember it's just pitch and catch. And picture London's face in the catcher's mitt."

We stepped onto the grass. London's face would most definitely be transposed to that mitt. That image garnered half of a smile.

Jerrick Locke rounded the snack shack and headed our direction. This morning, Cayla and I found the guts to say hi and ask if he was coming to our game today. That was all we had the nerve to do. He was six-foot, one inch. An inch taller than Roan. Since I was five-foot-ten, I noticed the height of boys I dreamed about dating.

When Jerrick was on the baseball team, he pitched and caught. Word was he got kicked off the team last year because he got into it with the coach...more than once. Roan thought Jerrick pushed it too far, maybe even wanted Coach to kick him off. Jerrick had some family issues. He might still, but he was one good-looking bad boy.

Jerrick lifted his chin in that guy greeting way and said, "Martin." He held a giant pretzel in one hand and a soda in the other.

"Locke," Roan grumbled. He always grumbled. "What are you doing here?"

Jerrick's gaze moved to mine and then over my uniform. I wasn't good at style, but it didn't take a genius to see a softball uniform made me look more like a guy. "Thought I'd watch the mighty Lionesses in action. I hear Tommie is tough from the circle."

Heat spread from my cheeks to my ears. I glanced down, not sure what to say.

Roan shifted his weight, moving a bit closer to me. "She's the best. But Mazzie's on today."

I turned to Roan, giving him a scowl. What was he trying to do, get Jerrick to leave?

"Heard they got three steals on you over the weekend. You need me to give you some pointers?" Jerrick grinned and took a bite of his pretzel.

"I'm good," Roan deadpanned.

Jerrick smirked and sauntered toward the Lions' softball stands. "You'll be warming up, won't you, Tommie?"

I nodded. Why didn't my words work around him?

His eyes lingered on me for a few more steps.

"I can't believe it." I watched Jerrick move like sexy molasses to the metal bleachers.

"What?" Roan asked.

"Cayla and I asked him to come to the game. Eek!" I bounced on my toes as a happy dance. "He's here."

"Don't," Roan said as if he was giving me an order.

"Don't what?" I looked up at him with my eyebrows knit together. The smack of a fast-pitched softball hitting the glove drew my attention to the field.

"Don't go after Jerrick. Promise me," he said.

"I need to get over there and warm up before I get in trouble." I took a step, but Roan latched onto the back of my jersey. I stopped and looked back over my shoulder at him.

"Promise me," he said.

I tried to step away, but he wouldn't let go. "Why? Then you won't have to help me."

"I'm not letting you go until you promise."

I shrugged and said, "Only if you promise to help me

find someone better."

He tugged the jersey, pulling me closer, and mumbled near my ear, "I promise I'll think about it."

Warm-up pitches were happening, and I needed to get my butt over there or I'd be higher on Coach's crap list. "Okay...I have to go." He held on. I sighed and gave him the word he was waiting for. "Promise." I didn't need the coach to chew my butt in front of Jerrick for being late.

He released my jersey, and I jogged off toward the dugout.

He called, "Good luck on the game."

I spun around and jogged backward as I pointed my glove at him. "You too!"

He headed for his field and I spun back around, jogging behind the bleachers to the dugout.

Coach Mac was already there. "Nice of you to join us, Tommie."

Keeping my mouth shut was the best answer, so I hung up my bag and fished a ball out. As I stepped onto the dirt from the concrete, I glanced up at the stands and saw Jerrick kicking back. He had sunglasses on, so I couldn't tell where he was looking exactly. When I turned to join Mazzie and Summer, Roan's large form passed outside the outfield fence.

Maybe Jerrick showing up was just the kick in the pants Roan needed.

"Hey, Juju girl. Are you going to study with me?" My cute little pug lifted her head from her comfy curled-up position on the floor at the end of my bed. She'd followed me upstairs after I got home from practice.

I closed my door and dug in my drawer for a pair of comfy shorts and a Lions softball T-shirt. The much-needed shower had cooled me off from practice.

After I dressed and hung my towel up, I scooped Juju in my arms and flopped on my bed. I turned on my side, flicking my damp hair out of my face, and stroked her back. "Practice was good for once, Juju Bead. Today's the first time in a while I didn't need to ice my shoulder. And the first time Coach didn't chew me out after practice in what seems like a month."

After Roan pointed out what I was doing wrong

yesterday, I was able to get back into my groove. Picturing London's gossipy face in the catcher's mitt... bullseye every time. I wondered how his practice went.

I snatched my phone off of my nightstand to send him a message. He'd sent me one while I was in the shower.

Roan: You need help studying tonight?

That was his way of rubbing my face in the fact he didn't have homework and only had one test to study for this week. I let his comment slide.

Tommie: How was practice?

When we had our pitch and catch session, the only thing I saw off was his toes weren't pointing out far enough when receiving the ball. He wanted me to take some video of the next game. Not sure if that would happen.

Roan: Better. I'm in your kitchen.

"Roan's here, girl." I scratched behind Juju's ears. "You want to go see him?

She talked to me in growly whines. Cayla thought it

was weird, but what she didn't understand was Juju totally got me.

I lifted her off the bed and sat her on the light gray carpet. "Let's go, girl. Maybe you could bite his ankle until he agrees to help me find a kissing tutor?"

She barked once.

I giggled and opened my door. "I'll take that as a yes."

When I asked him about it this morning, he said he was still thinking about it. All he had to do was drop subtle hints that he knew someone looking for a no-strings-attached make-out partner. How hard could it be?

We followed the hall to the stairwell. Halfway down, the pungent aroma of asparagus cooking hit me. I liked the vegetable, but my sister hated it. Little Miss Perfect was probably holed up in her room, gagging.

Served her right after her not-so-subtle hints that my wardrobe was part of my problem. She said, "Guys don't go out with girls who dress like guys." And then she proved her point by going through my closet and dresser.

It wasn't fair she got the best of everything from our family's DNA. Brains, looks, athleticism, older boys interested in dating her. But ever since she was in junior high, she had talked down to me like I was stupid, and she was better than me. Just because I didn't make straight A's didn't mean I was stupid.

The thought of Mom making her eat a bite and Madi

gagging as soon as it hit her tongue caused me to snicker. "This is turning out to be a good day."

After I hopped to the floor from the bottom step, I crossed through the construction zone of a living room. Mom had stripped the wall that stood between the kitchen and living room down to the studs. She had wiring that needed moved and a reinforcement beam installed. Even the floor was down to bare plywood.

Her hobby was part of the reason she worked part-time at the hospital. That was on top of her regular job as a nurse at the Women's Wellness Center. Which meant Mom worked a lot. I think she stayed so busy, so she didn't miss Dad. At least that's what Aunt Ginny told me last year when she came to visit.

Roan's grandpa's laughter filled the air of the first floor. My smile widened. He had a great laugh. Hearty and full of life. Roan's could be just as contagious when he let go.

I peered through the two-by-fours and saw Roan cutting veggies at the chopping block. He knew his way around a kitchen.

Our eyes met. His full lips curled into a smile, and he lifted a hand in a wave.

Mom stirred something in a pot at the stove. The aroma told me it was mashed potatoes. She glanced my direction after Roan waved. "There she is," she said. She always made sure to take Wednesdays and Sunday mornings off. Almost always.

Roan rarely missed Wednesday nights except during baseball season. Sometimes he had games, or I had games.

"Are we having a party? On a school night, even?" I teased, crossing the old threshold between the rooms.

Jim turned toward me. "Tommie, my dear, we need a babysitter for a few days."

I giggled, locking on to Roan's face as he shook his head and rolled his eyes. Yes, he totally rolled his eyes. "Oh, yeah?" I asked and leaned my forearms against the countertop at the island across from Roan. "How much are you paying? You know what a pain in the butt this kid is."

Jim cleared his throat, drawing my attention back to him. He leaned over as if we had a private negotiation going on. "Fifty's a fair price, don't you think?" he asked in a serious tone.

"If you're talking fifty an hour," I shot back.

Jim broke out in a laugh. Roan kept his unfazed expression, chopping along. Now that I was closer, I determined he was making a salad.

"All right, you two," Marilyn cut in. "Roan doesn't find you very amusing."

I rounded the island and chimed, "He always finds

me amusing." I pulled a salad bowl out of the cabinet and sat it next to the chopping board. "Right, Roan?"

He grunted in response, so I poked at his ticklish spots until he danced around.

"Hey," he said. "I'm working with a knife here."

"I better check the grill." Jim chuckled, lifting the platter and tongs off of the countertop, and headed for the back door. We kept our grill on the back deck right outside the kitchen.

"Gramp's brother is having surgery at the end of the week. He and Grandma are going out of town for a few days. He says I'm irresponsible and need a babysitter," Roan said with a shake of his head.

Marilyn stood across from us. Her thin frame and aristocratic stature seemed out of place with me, Roan, and, the construction zone in the room. She shook her head and said, "We just want to make sure you eat well and don't throw a party while we're gone."

"You know I can take care of myself," he grumbled.

"A home-cooked dinner every night would be nice, wouldn't it?" Mom asked. She knew how much Roan loved good food. Or food period. But good food was a bonus.

I reached my arm around his waist and laid my head against his beefy arm.

He paused his pepper dicing. I saw his lips part with a bigger smile.

"We can make a tent like old times," I said with a hint of nostalgia. When we were kids, his grandparents sometimes went on weekend trips without Roan. He would stay with us. Usually in my room, and we rigged up a blanket tent to sleep in.

His body shook with a chuckle, but he said nothing.

MADI, ROAN, AND I CLEANED UP THE KITCHEN FROM dinner, and we said goodbye to Roan's grandparents. They assured Roan they'd only be gone a few nights.

After they left, Roan carried Juju upstairs to my room so he could help me study for our last English test before final exams. That pug purred like a kitten when he held her against his chest. Traitor. She was supposed to bite his ankle, not cuddle with him.

I snatched my computer out of my bag, found a seat on the floor, and logged into our English study guide. "Are you going to help me, or what?"

"Yeah, hand me the laptop." He slid down the wall to the floor next to me and sat Juju between us.

I groaned. "You know that's not what I'm talking about." He hadn't mentioned a word about helping me find a kissing tutor since he said he'd think about it.

He shrugged, staring at me with his best innocent expression. "What are you talking about, then?"

It was obvious he didn't think the idea was brilliant when I first brought it up. And if it got out that I needed someone to teach me how to kiss, leaving town to never return would be the only option. But this could absolutely work. My insides crawled with excitement over knowing how crucial the right tutor was to the success of finding my very own boyfriend. If I got a bad tutor...ugh. It could lead to failure and possibly another round of public humiliation.

I backhanded him in the gut. *Ouch*. I rubbed my hand. That was a bad idea. His stomach was like a rock. "Are you going to help me find a kissing tutor or not?"

His head thumped against the wall. "Toms," he said in a groan.

"Roans," I whined, mimicking him.

He shot me a sideways glare. That was a thing with him. He knew how to make others cower at his brooding appearance, but it didn't work on me.

"Fine," I sang. "Jerrick seemed like he might be interested in me at the game. If that doesn't work out, I could stalk Olivia Matthews for a couple of days and do what she does." Not that I knew if a guy was interested. That wasn't a natural ability for me, unlike Cayla, Madi, Summer, and at least three-fourths of the softball team.

He folded his arms tight against his chest. His dark hair fell along his eyebrow. The tips had lightened from the sun. How such dark hair could get sun streaks the color of his eyes eluded me, but it happened every year.

He tried to change the direction of our conversation. "Since you're babysitting me while my grandparents are gone, I expect to be entertained."

"Don't I always entertain you?"

I handed the computer over, stood, and crossed the room to my bed. Between all the pillows and my plush headboard, it was the most comfortable spot in my room. I snatched up a pillow to hug and plopped down, scooting against the headboard.

He wore a smirk on his face while he situated the laptop on his legs. When he looked up at me, his amber eyes were dancing. "Sometimes you just annoy me."

He was irresistible when his playful side came out. It felt like flirting, but what did I know about that? A bubble grew in my chest. The kind that was full of fun and laughter and something confusing... butterflies. I did my best to ignore it and shot him a smirk. "The feeling's mutual. Like now." I threw one of the small pillows at him. "Are you going to help me find a tutor or not?"

Juju lifted her head from her curled-up position beside him and barked in agreement.

Roan broke eye contact with me, propped the pillow behind him, and looked down at the screen. His voice softened. "Let's study. I promise we'll talk about it tomorrow."

8

The aroma of melted cheese, cooked eggs, and tomatoes filled my nostrils as Roan slid the omelet in front of me. "Mmm, this smells amazing."

The corners of his mouth pulled up. "Protein-powered breakfast is the best." He turned back to the stove and readied the skillet for his egg mixture. Roan didn't need help taking care of himself like his grandpa teased. For an eighteen-year-old-boy, he was a good cook. He even knew how to do laundry.

Roan sent me a message after he left last night to come over for breakfast before he drove me to school. We used to do this before our games last year, but it was the first time this season. Hopefully, he was ready to commit to finding me a kissing tutor, or Cayla and I would have to take things into our own hands.

I had even considered getting James alone and asking

him for some private lessons. Public scenes didn't work out for us, but maybe a few private kissing sessions would do the trick and he would want me to be his girl-friend. Who was I kidding? I couldn't even face the guy to apologize for the whole thing, for leaving him in the middle of the dance floor.

I cut into the omelet and pulled a forkful up to my lips. My mouth was already watering. I shoved a bite in my mouth. "Mmm," I moaned, letting my lids slide shut as I chewed. "Perfection."

When I came back to the moment, Roan had plated his omelet and stared at me. The playful grin and dancing eyes from last night were back. Just when I thought he would shoot me a smart-aleck comment, he said, "I know someone who would be a good tutor for you." He rounded the island and sat beside on the bar stool next to mine.

It took me a second to process. I blinked my eyes, not sure I heard him correctly. "You do?"

He nodded, cutting his food into bite-sized pieces. "But you agree that whatever I say goes." He glanced at me before taking a bite.

I took a drink of my milk. Roan liked being in control. It was fun to disrupt his bossy pants. It had become my mission to throw him off his throne. This was him snipping my chances of doing exactly that.

My insides tightened. Did I really want to agree to him bossing me around with no pushback? "Why?"

"It's all about trust." He put his fork down and focused on me, asking, "Do you trust me?"

I knew exactly what he was doing. He pulled this trick with his pitchers. It was how he got them settled down and back in their pitching groove.

"Look, you know guys. And you have a way of getting your way. Which is why I asked for your help in the first place. But I'm not one of your pitchers you can control." Allowing someone else to have total control picking out the lips I'd have close personal contact with didn't seem like a good plan. Even if it was a friend as good as Roan.

"All you have to do is say yes, and you can start today," he said with an unaffected tone.

Did he talk to some guys last night after he left my house? I cleared my throat. "Who?"

"You don't need to worry about that."

I swiveled on the barstool to face him. "Uh, yeah, I do. They can't have a girlfriend," I pointed out, hoping he'd drop a name or a hint of who it was.

"That's a given. Don't worry. I've heard first-hand that girls find him attractive. I have everything covered. If you agree, you're in. No turning back."

I narrowed my eyes. In one night, he had all the bases covered? He had to have either planned this for longer than one day or thought about it all night long. Which I highly doubted since he appeared to be well rested and very well put together this morning.

He went back to eating and so did I. After I finished, I took my plate to the sink, rinsed it off, and placed it in the dishwasher. Though my mind buzzed with the faces of guys Roan might have lined up, my sister's comments about my clothes had me wondering if it would even work. "Madi told me I needed to change my wardrobe. She said I need to dress more 'feminine.'" I stood before him, watching his eyes scrutinize me. "Is she right?"

He shrugged. "It wouldn't hurt. Maybe switch up the athletic gear some."

I pursed my lips and groaned. Sometimes he was too honest. "I was afraid of that." My throat tightened. I knew guys didn't see me as a girl or think I was pretty because they never asked me out.

I had to talk Roan into helping me find a prom date, for Pete's sake. I slumped over on the countertop and said, "We're going shopping after the game tonight. I hate shopping. Clothes never fit right." Maybe it would be worth it. I straightened and asked again, "Who is it? Have you already talked to them?"

He kept his grin and raised an eyebrow. "You haven't agreed yet."

Roan wouldn't stick me with a jerk. I tossed my

hands up. "Fine. Agree. Whatever. Let's get the tutor scheduled."

"Okay." He stood, pulled a paper and pen out of his back pocket, unfolded the paper, and placed them on the countertop in front of me. "Sign on the dotted line."

I scoffed. "What's this?" I scanned the paper. A contract?

"No backing out," he said. "If I agree to help with this, you have to do what I say. And you know I wouldn't do something mean."

I rolled my eyes. "I never knew you wanted to be a lawyer like Gramps."

He pointed to the paper.

I let out a growl, but I knew I had to do it. I snatched the pen and scribbled my signature on the paper. He'd already signed by his name. "There. Done. Who's my tutor?"

He stepped closer, looking into my eyes with the same expression he had when he'd said he found some-one. "Me."

I laughed out loud. He had to be joking. But when he didn't join with me, I choked on my laughter. "What?" My face pinched, but my belly went on a rollercoaster ride.

"I'm more than capable of teaching a girl how to kiss."

I backed away, but he followed me until I bumped into the cabinets. I stuttered, "You can't. We can't."

"Why not?" he asked. His eyes bore into me. He had looked at me like that before, and it made my belly quiver like it was doing at that very moment.

"Because we've been best friends since we were ten, that's why." I gripped the edge of the counter and pressed my back against it.

"Eight," he said softly, brushing his fingers on my cheek as he tucked a piece of my hair behind my ear. When I came over that morning, I was in a rush and hadn't put it in a ponytail yet. "Best friends are more comfortable with each other." His voice was tender and smooth and, combined with his touch, it made my stomach dip again.

"It's embarrassing," I said in a weak, unsure voice.

"You agreed. Even signed a legally binding document." He leaned his head down. "We should get started on our first lesson."

A huge lump stuck in my throat, causing my mouth to go dry. I didn't even think my lungs were working. *Tommie, you can't kiss your best friend.* I frantically shook my head.

He chuckled, leaning even closer. "You want to learn to be a good kisser, right?"

I pressed my palms against his chest. "Yeah, but I...I want to do it with someone that...likes me."

"I like you just fine." He lingered for a moment before he straightened and stepped away. Roan lifted his backpack from the chair across the room and said, "We should get to school."

There was no way Roan could be my kissing tutor. He just said I didn't dress like a girl, and even though it might be true, it hurt. This was a joke to him. Pressure pushed in on my chest. It was like I was reliving the day after prom and everyone was still laughing at me.

Didn't he get it? Finding someone to boost my reputation in the love department wasn't a joke.

"You coming?" he asked, heading for the door as if he didn't just stomp on my hopes of fixing my reputation and changing how guys looked at me.

I lifted my chin, strode to the door, and picked up my pack where I'd dropped it when I first arrived. If it wasn't getting so late, I'd message Cayla to have her pick me up.

I climbed in Roan's truck and put on my seatbelt.

Two seconds later, he slid in and started the engine, backed out of the driveway, and headed to school. Halfway there, he asked, "You okay?"

"You being my tutor is not going to work." Even if Roan had turned on the hot factor, along with a dozen other guys this year, I was his buddy. Tommie, the tomboy. The girl who taught him how to play baseball. No guy found that attractive. Especially one who'd been friends with me for so long. Knowing he would be grossed out while he was trying to teach me was one more humiliation I didn't want to go through.

"It's too late to back out. What I say goes, remember?"

Cayla was not going to believe this, and I wasn't sure I would tell her.

9

Throughout school, I pretended everything was fine. Roan always knew how to put his issues aside and focus on the task at hand. If he could do it, so could I. With a test to study for and an essay due, I needed to forget the morning conversation with Roan ever happened. Thinking about his stupid contract would land me an F.

"Tommie, I don't think I've ever seen you so focused," Madi said, hanging another shirt over the dressing room door. "It was like the crowd didn't even exist."

I'd had a smile on my face since the game ended, but Madi's compliment was like the chocolate frosting on top. She didn't give them to me often.

Since I proved my pitching was back on track yesterday, Coach started me in the game. It went better than expected. "Yeah, it was almost mechanical. I just served it where it needed to go."

"See, you are a beast. When are you going to listen to me?" Cayla added. "Maybe we should have gone to the guys' game after ours."

I hadn't said a word to Cayla about Roan's little stunt this morning. Truthfully, I wasn't sure it hadn't been a bad dream. I slipped a flirty pink top over my head and looked in the mirror. The high from winning the game plummeted. I mumbled, "Too bad I look like a beast too." Why did they use florescent lights in tiny dressing rooms?

"Let us see," Madi called.

I turned the handle as she pulled the door open.

Judging by their faces, I wasn't the only one with that assessment.

I lifted my arms out to the sides. "See why I hate shopping? At least my athletic shorts and T-shirts fit."

Madi planted her hands on her waist, pushing her hip out, and cocked her head to the side. "They don't fit. They hang on you like a garbage bag." She pointed to the third outfit I tried on. "This isn't the right style for you. This is exactly why you should try on clothes."

I rolled my eyes and went back in the dressing room to strip. "The next thing I put on better work or I'm done."

"We'll find what works for you," Madi tried to soothe me. "I have an idea. Give me a minute."

"Why am I even doing this?" Tears stung my eyes as I shoved the skirt to the floor and stared at myself again. I turned away, sniffing back the emotion, and wrapped my arms around my middle. Any space this tiny box had seemed to close in on me.

"Hey, Tommie?" Cayla asked softly.

I was grouchy—I knew that. It was just...ugh, trying on clothes always put me in a bad mood. And I could no longer keep this morning's events out of my mind. Stacking those two things on top of each other made me want to curl up on my bed with Juju and binge-watch movies on my phone for the rest of the night. "Yeah?"

"Let's just forget about Roan," she said. "If he doesn't want to help, we can do this ourselves."

A couple of drops of salty liquid slid down my cheek. I should tell her. I needed someone to commiserate with. I wiped the wetness from my face and cleared my throat. "This morning, Roan said he'd help me."

"What? Why didn't you say anything?" she asked.

Maybe I hoped it would just go away. I shrugged. I didn't know why because she couldn't see me through the door. "I don't think I want to do this anymore. There's only, what? A month left of school?"

I saw her sneakers under the door turn to face my

direction. "That's silly. If Roan will help, it'll make this go quicker."

"Cayla, he said if I agreed, I had to do it his way."

"So? I might think he's an intimidating jerk sometimes, but he's not to you. And he wouldn't recruit someone who would treat you bad or he didn't trust."

I pushed out a frustrated breath. "He said *he* would be my tutor." I stared down at my bare feet. Chipped polish and nails. They were a mess, just like me.

My words hung in the air. If it weren't for seeing her aqua-colored Chuck Taylors under the dressing room door, I would've thought she left.

"Okay, I found some things I think you'll like." Madi laid them over the top of the door. "Try on the dress first. I know you don't like dresses, but this will be so comfortable. Promise." She switched gears, asking Cayla, "What's going on?"

"I'm not sure," Cayla said. "If I heard your sister correctly, she found herself a hot kissing tutor, but now she wants to back out of it."

"What? When? Who is it?" Madi asked in rapid fire. "Why do you want to back out?"

I gripped the hook of the hangers for the clothes that draped over the door and hung them on the peg mounted on the wall. I mumbled an answer. "Because it's not going to work." I untangled the cotton dress and slipped it over my head.

Cayla told her, "Roan said he'd do it."

Madi's sandals clapped against the floor as she jumped up and down. She squealed and said, "Oh, my gosh! Tommie! This is fantastic!"

"I know, right?" Cayla cheered with Madi.

"He's one of my best friends. How am I supposed to kiss him?" I looked in the mirror and tried to wrap a piece of fabric from the dress, but it didn't look right. "How does this thing work?" I opened the door.

Cayla's eyes widened, followed by her mouth dropping open. "That looks perfect."

"You take this strap." Madi looped it behind me. "See? It wraps around and then you tie it on the side." She took a step back, wearing a toothy smile. "Your boobs look bigger."

"Ooh,,it's the pin stripes," Cayla said. "They curve in all the right places. It makes your hips look curvy too." Her eyes were as big as softballs. "And your eyes... the green is breathtaking."

Madi giggled. "I know. This lavender is perfect. Roan will flip when he sees you in this. Definitely a yes."

I scowled. "I can't."

Cayla stepped in front of me and took my hands in hers, asking, "I know you think he's good-looking. It was his idea. Why can't you?"

I dropped my gaze. With every thought and word about Roan, my chest weighed heavier. "Yeah, he's tall, dark, and handsome. And I even get that nervous twist in my stomach when I'm around him sometimes, but he doesn't see me like that. I'm just one of the guys." My throat tightened. Admitting this out loud was one more drop of humiliation in my rapidly expanding lake. I glanced around the dressing area. There had been a woman trying clothes on earlier, but I didn't see her.

"It's just us," Cayla said, releasing my hands.

My teeth grazed my bottom lip before I continued, "I had hoped the tutor would turn into a boyfriend or at least a few sweet dates in public where I got caught looking like an expert kisser. Not like I was mauling my prey."

Madi snickered. "You've really become dramatic this year."

I puffed out a shot of air through my nostrils as one corner of my mouth lifted. It eased the pressure from my chest too. That seemed to be true. This whole year had been a rollercoaster ride. "Maybe," I admitted.

My phone dinged from the shorts pocket I'd worn to the store. They hung on one of the pegs in the dressing room.

"Look," Cayla said, tilting her head. "If Roan didn't want to do this, he never would have offered. He's probably been stewing over it since the moment you asked. Just give it a try."

"Yeah, sis. Maybe you two are meant to be together.

Wouldn't that be awesome?" She clasped her hands together with a dreamy look in her eyes. "I hope one day I can fall in love with a boy who's my best friend."

"Me too." Cayla wrapped her arms around me. Madi joined the group hug.

"Ugh, I'm not in love with him. He's not in love with me."

"Just see how it goes. If it's weird after he kisses you a couple times, all you have to do is say so. Okay?" she asked.

"You could be in love and not realize it," Madi said with a hopeful voice. "But even if you're not, you get to practice with a hot guy. Roan fits that description."

I closed my eyes and groaned. They were right. I was running out of time. "I'll try it."

The girls untangled themselves. Madi turned on her bossy voice and said, "Try on the other outfit."

I stepped back in the confined space, closed the door, and pressed the lock button on the handle. I dared to check my reflection. A smile stretched across my face. The dress fit my body in all the right ways. I looked good. And definitely like a girl.

"That dress is on the sporty side. And so is the rest of what I picked out. Let me get a pair of shoes to go with it." Madi's sandals clopped away.

"You want me to message Roan that you're ready to get started?" Cayla asked.

I slipped the dress off and tossed it over the top of the door. "No," I said quickly. "I'll talk to him." It was hard to say what Cayla would send him, thinking she was helping.

I pulled on a pair of shorts. Even though I had no problem buttoning them, they clung to my body and were shorter than I usually wore. I grasped the hem and tugged them down. The shirt seemed okay. I slid my hands through the armholes and lifted it over my head. It had more of an hourglass shape to it rather than the usual straight T-shirt I was accustomed to.

I opened the door. "Well?" I turned in a circle. "The shorts are too tight."

"They're perfect!" Madi grabbed my shoulders and spun me around again.

Cayla gave me two thumbs up. "They seriously show off your legs," she said.

Showing my legs off was not a good thing. My phone dinged again. I'd forgotten to check it. "One more outfit and I'm done trying on clothes."

I closed the door and dug my phone out of the shorts I'd worn here. Now that I was aware, they were basically basketball shorts. Ugh, I needed to change it up a little. I typed in my code and checked my messages.

Roan: Heard you had a great game. Let's celebrate. Pick you up in ten minutes?

Roan: I'm at your house. Where are you?

My stomach did that rollercoaster dip like the other night and I wasn't even in his presence. "Roan said he heard I had a good game and wants to celebrate," I said, but it came out as a question. If he was my kissing tutor, he might plan to kiss me. The thought made my insides jittery. What had I agreed to?

Cayla shot me an order. "Tell him you will meet him at the pier."

Before thinking about it, I typed the message and pressed send.

"Hurry and try on the last outfit," Madi barked. Now my little sister was giving me orders? Was everyone in charge except me?

I changed clothes while they were muttering to each other. If my pulse wasn't beating like a base drum in my ears, I might have been able to understand what they were talking about.

I pulled on the white, straight-legged pants and tied the drawstring. The coral shirt was tight and a little on the bright side for me, but obviously I wasn't good at style. "Okay," I said, turning the handle and stepping out.

"Dang, Tommie." Cayla's eyes widened with her smile. "You look amazing."

I giggled. "Good thing I have on white underwear today."

"Here," Madi said, handing me the sandals. "Put these on."

I slipped on the nude-colored shoes. They were comfortable. I looked down at the top. "This shirt isn't too...tight and bright?"

"Just because you can tell you have boobs doesn't mean it's too tight. And the color goes with your skin tone." Madi pointed at my waist. "Tuck it in though."

After I did as she said, she moved her finger in a circle, directing me to turn around.

I did as she asked. Again.

She and Cayla smacked high fives and bumped hips. "Mission accomplished!" Madi stepped closer, grabbed the price tags, and snapped the plastic from the shirt and pants.

"What are you doing?" She knew better than to steal. Didn't she?

She held them up and said, "You're wearing this on your first tutoring session."

"It's not an official lesson. We're celebrating our wins. We do this all the time," I explained. It was more for my benefit than theirs.

Cayla had snuck behind me and gathered the clothes I'd worn in. "You're not getting these back. Not today anyway." She did hand over my phone though and I slid it in the pants pocket.

"Let me fix your hair." Madi slipped a comb out of

her purse and pulled my hair into a messy bun. "Just need a little..." She dug in her purse and took out a stick of eyeliner, a tube of mascara, and lip gloss. "Enhancement," she finished and began to apply the color my top eyelids by my lashes. Nothing like a pointy stick near the eye. I insisted on doing the mascara myself. I'd done it a few times. Putting on the lip gloss was a no brainer.

"What all do you have in the purse?" I teased. My phone dinged. I pulled the phone from my pocket and checked the message. My heart beat increased. I swallowed and said, "He's there."

All three of us squealed. What was wrong with me? This was Roan, my best friend, not one of my Sweet Water High crushes.

"Okay. It's just another day. You're just wearing different clothes. That's it," Cayla assured me.

I nodded, hoping she was right. I took in a steadying breath. "Thanks, guys," I said. Maybe if Roan could see that I could look nice, like a girl, other boys would too.

Madi gathered the other outfit. "Let's pay and get you to the beach."

10

Cayla slowed at the curb by the pier, practically kicked me out of the Jeep, and sped off. It might have had something to do with me deciding I should send Roan a message saying I didn't feel good and that I had gone home.

While I stood at the edge of the wide concrete separating the road and the sand, I swallowed and took a few slow breaths to calm my racing heart. An older couple holding hands passed in front of me. I took another deep breath and told myself, *it's just you and Roan. No big deal. You celebrate like this all the time.*

Scanning the cars parked along the road, I spotted Roan's gray Toyota truck two cars down, but he wasn't in it. My search moved across the few people on the beach and those lining the pier, fishing. Roan's back and wide shoulders caught my eye at the end of the long dock. A tiny shot of adrenaline spiked through my chest as if I was about to do something completely wild and dangerous.

The rush of the ocean tide usually relaxed me, so I closed my eyes for a second and listened. Sweet Water was such a great place to grow up. Sand and surf anytime I wanted. Good friends to share it with. And softball.

My pulse had settled. A calm confidence came over me. I opened my eyes to begin my trek and saw that Roan headed toward me. His dark hair lifted from the ocean breeze. It didn't matter what time of year it was. His complexion made him look tanned. In the pictures I'd seen of his mom, she had dark hair too, but her light skin was more like mine. His dad had bronzed skin. I suppose that had to do with him being from Argentina.

Roan had on a small grin as he approached. He was wearing loafers too, which meant we wouldn't be going to the batting cages. My attire wouldn't work for something like that. When we were only a few feet away, his eyes widened and the grin he was wearing faded for a brief moment.

My stomach dropped. The girls wouldn't lie to me about looking nice, would they? I stopped and waited for him, trying to smile. "Hey," I said.

He stopped in front of me with his eyebrows lifted. He chuckled. "I almost didn't recognize you. New clothes?" he asked, looking me over.

"Yep." I shuffled my weight from one foot to the other. "So, how was your game?"

"You weren't there," he grumbled.

I shoved my hands in my pockets. "Uh, Cayla, Madi, and I went shopping. Hence the new clothes."

"Ah." He nodded toward the sidewalk, held his arm out, and waited for me to step that direction. We walked side by side. "We won. I did okay."

I fixed my eyes on his expression and asked, "Just okay? What happened?"

He shrugged. "My stance was okay. I felt...off. You know?"

I had plenty of feeling off lately. I nodded. "What do you think it is? Coach on your case?"

"Nah, it's not that." He paused. Shrugged. "My grandparents might downsize. My dad called and wants me to come visit." He tilted his head up and let out a long breath.

"After all this time of silence? He's got a lot of nerve." Roan was a big boy who can take care of himself. I knew that. But when it came to protecting his heart from his dad, I was like a mamma bear. "Tell him he lost his privileges when he left. That jerk."

"Yeah, I know. Grams thinks it might be a good idea, but Gramps doesn't. He's concerned if I go to Argentina, he might try to get me to stay. He said the government could keep me from traveling back, and I would be stuck there." He led us to a bench overlooking the beach and sea.

I took a seat and he settled next to me. "Do you want to go?" I wouldn't have thought traveling to see his dad was even a thought after all this time.

"I don't know." He stretched his arms on either side of him along the back of the bench. "I have so many questions, but I'd like the satisfaction of telling him off to his face."

"Make him come and see you," I said. Roan, his dad, and grandparents moved here right after his mom died. His grandparents had lived in Sweet Water before and liked the town. When Roan and his dad moved in with them, they decided they needed a bigger house and better schools. That's when he came into my life.

"Yeah," he said, sounding unsure. "That's probably what I'll do."

I swiveled on the bench and angled toward him. Roan was decisive. But when it came to his dad, all bets were off. "You still have that punching bag hanging in your garage, don't you?" I asked.

"Yeah" he said with his eyebrows knit together. "Why?"

"I think we ought to start training. If your dad shows," I smacked my fist into my palm, "I'm going to punch him right in the nose."

Roan busted up, laughing. "You couldn't punch your way out of a paper bag."

"Oh, yeah?" I asked, jabbing him in the stomach.

He grabbed my wrists and put on a shocked expression. "You're so violent," he teased. "I'm not sure I can tutor someone with that kind of behavior."

I gave him a giant eye roll, hoping he didn't notice the heat flushing my neck and cheeks.

He stood, continued chuckling at me, and pulled me up by my wrist with him and said, "Come on. I haven't been on the beach in a while. Let's walk along the surf."

"No football, or Frisbee?" Usually we had something to do besides walk.

He shook his head and slipped his shoes off.

I leaned down and rolled up my pant legs to my calves, slipped my sandals off, and hooked my fingers through the back straps. I hoped he didn't notice my shoddy toenails. "I'm ready," I said.

The warm sand relaxed me even when I thought I was already there. We stepped through the grains and walked along the tide. The direction we took was the opposite of people and the busyness of the shops along the waterfront.

Roan bumped my shoulder and said, "Sorry, didn't plan on moping about my dad. Tell me about your win."

"Don't worry about it," I said, wrapping my hands

around his arm and leaning my head on his shoulder. "That's what best friends are for." I let our closeness sink in for a moment before I straightened. "Pitching felt good. It was almost like I was a pitching machine. My stride was the same every time." I looked up at him. "Thanks for that." Roan pointed that out to me right away the other morning. How could he figure that out in three pitches but my coach couldn't tell me what I was doing wrong?

"What can I say? I know you." He beamed.

I giggled and teased, "Aren't you glad you moved next to Tommie the Tomboy? I totally rocked your world."

He chuckled as he slung his arm around my shoulders and said, "You did rock my world. Twice. I don't know what I would've done without you when we moved in, or when Dad left."

My eyes watered and I blinked to keep any tears from falling. The breeze helped dry them up too. How did he go from teasing to heart-wrenching so fast? It gave me emotional whiplash.

"You do the same for me." Dad had either been deployed or away for training with the Marines most of my life. I hardly got to talk to him because of the time difference. This was getting depressing. I had to change the gloom. "What should we do to celebrate? I was pretty awesome," I said teasingly. I jumped in front of him and did an impression of his little hip action he does after catching the last pitch of a winning game.

It didn't last long because he lugged me over his shoulder and ran down the beach. "You're getting launched into the water."

"Okay," I squealed, laughing so hard I snorted. "I'll stop. I'll stop."

"I'm going to teach you a lesson," he said, wading out a few feet into the water.

Giggles kept pouring out of me to the point my cheeks hurt, and I was gasping for air.

He back-stepped to the edge of the lapping tide and slid me off his shoulder onto the shifting sand. Strands of my hair fell out of the bun on top my head, but I was having too much fun to care about what I looked like.

Roan kept his grip on my waist. His chest rose and fell as fast as mine. I knew this because, for some reason, my palms pressed against his pecs.

I couldn't look away. He was so...pretty. Thick-chested men could definitely be pretty. His warm eyes glanced at my mouth before he leaned down. My heart raced even faster than it was.

"I'm going to kiss you," he whispered, his warm breath brushing my skin before our mouths met.

Heat spread across my lips and down to my heart. Instead of being rigid like the night James kissed me, I softened, melting against Roan. This was so much better.

Roan's lips were not too soft, not too tight. They were just right.

He pulled away before I was ready. "Lesson one. Kissing is better when it's spontaneous."

Oh, it was a tutoring lesson. I looked down at his embroidered eagle on his cotton polo. My excited heart down-shifted. It didn't realize his kiss wasn't real either. I separated myself from him. My body didn't want to obey though, so I had to take another step back.

Forcing my eyes to steer clear of his, I tried to act like I knew it wasn't real. "I see. Spontaneous. Right. Lesson one." I cleared my throat, stuffing my hands in my pants pockets.

"You want to go to the Burger Bar and get something to eat?" he asked.

I turned back to the direction we came from. "I can't. I should get back since it's my night to cook."

"Oh," he said with surprise. "Okay."

The stroll back to his truck was more like a speed-walk. The kind middle-aged women that raced by my house three times a week did, pumping their bent arms back and forth in rapid motion. We climbed in his truck and he started the engine as we buckled our seat belts.

"Ready?" he asked. It was the first word either of us uttered since we left the beach.

I nodded.

His eyes scrolled down my new clothes and back,

lingering longer that I thought was normal for a friend before he pulled out onto the road. But what did I know?

When Roan turned on our street, he broke the silence between us and asked, "What are we having for supper?"

He wanted to come over? After the weirdness following his kiss? "Um, not sure. Something with hamburger. Probably a salad."

He stopped in front of my house. "I'll park my truck in the garage and be over to help."

That moment on the beach with him felt so real. I wanted it to be real, and that surprised me. This kissing tutor deal blurred the lines of friendship, and I wasn't sure I could separate the two. I wish Cayla was here to decipher what was going on.

11

Roan dried the table and rounded the island where I started the dishwasher. He tossed the towel by the sink and said, "Let's go get some gelato. You look too nice to hang out in the backyard."

My eyebrows might have shot clear off my forehead. Did I hear him right? When we got back from the beach, I just slipped an apron over my head to protect my clothes and got busy cooking. I glanced past Roan to my sister who was stepping out of the laundry room.

Her mouth dropped open before she covered it with her hand. And her eyes were as big as softballs. She lowered her hand and mouthed the words, "Say yes."

"Sure. Okay," I said.

He extended his arm, allowing me to walk out of the kitchen in front of him.

It wasn't until we stepped into Luigi's that the shock

wore off and I remembered I don't do public anymore. I paused at the door.

Roan's hand pressed against my back. "No one's here," he said, nudging me inside and toward the glass case with all the flavors.

It was dusk outside but was as bright as the noonday sun in the place. I could hear Tasha Martell's big bad wolf voice in my head. "The better to scrutinize you, my dear."

"What can I get you?" the older lady asked from behind the case.

"I'll have two scoops of chocolate suiza."

"You always get that," I teased, scanning the different flavors.

"That's because it's always good," he said. I could hear the smile in his voice. "I bet you're getting strawberry."

I shook my head and settled on one I hadn't had in a while. "Nope."

The gray-haired lady handed Roan his cup and asked, "What can I get you, sweetie?"

"A scoop of chocolate mousse, please," I said.

"Oh, that's a good one. I might have to steal a bite." He snagged a napkin and a spoon off the counter and dug into his gelato.

I watched him take a bite. A moan hummed out of him.

It caused a giggle to bubble out of me.

"Here you go, dear," the lady said.

I turned back to the counter and took the cup, giving her a smile, thanking her.

"I'll pay and we can sit outside and eat," he said, reaching for his wallet.

"Okay" I said, lifting a spoon from the tray, and headed toward the door.

I focused on scooping a spoonful of goodness when I bumped into a hard body and dropped my gelato on the floor. "Oh, I'm sorry," I apologized, kneeling down to scoop the blob back into the cup. That's when I saw chocolate streaks on my new white pants. Great.

"Tommie?" James Lowe's voice boomed down at me.

I glanced up at him. My eyes widened as he towered over me like a giant. I wanted to crawl across the black-and white -checkered floor and hide under a table.

"I haven't seen much of you since you left me standing in the middle of the dance floor at prom," James said. I couldn't tell if he was being mean or just speaking the truth. I avoided him at all costs at school. Which was also why I didn't go to Roan's games.

"That's enough, Lowe," Roan called, stepping next to me. He squatted down and handed me a few napkins, asking under his breath, "You okay?"

I nodded, took the napkins, and cleaned up the mess.

James' feet shuffled. "Hey, I just wanted to talk to her."

Roan stood, inching closer to James until they were toe to toe.

I stood and carried the mess to the trash can. My hands were sticky and I wanted to wash up in the bathroom, but the need to get out of there was stronger.

I pushed on the door and heard James call, "See you around."

I'm a big girl. Tall. Strong. But when it came to facing James Lowe, I shrunk to the size of a mouse.

I made it to the truck and waited for Roan to come out. The sun was about to disappear when we got here. Now it was dark enough for the streetlights to shine down. Darkness could hide the wet streaks streaming down my cheeks.

The door unlocked before I saw my friend. It took him longer than I thought it should, but I didn't say a word. The only thing I wanted to do was leave.

"Here." He held out a cup of chocolate mousse gelato. "I got you another one."

"Thanks. But you didn't have to." The truth was, I didn't have an appetite anymore.

He opened the door for me. "I know."

I climbed in and he shut the door behind me before rounding the truck to the driver's side.

Roan handed me his gelato and started the truck. "Mind holding on to that until we get home?"

"Sure," I mumbled.

Roan took off through town. I stared out the passenger window, thinking about my encounter. As small as I felt, it wasn't as bad as I thought it would be. He didn't laugh or make fishy lips or kissing noises. But that didn't mean I wanted to go through it again.

Before long, Roan pulled alongside my curb and parked. We stepped out of the cab, meeting in front of the truck. "I'm sorry about your new clothes," he said.

We moved side by side toward the house. "Hopefully Mom knows how to get the chocolate out."

Roan stopped me halfway to the front door. "Tommie Sue, you look real pretty tonight. Lowe made sure I knew he thought so too after you went outside."

"I don't look like a boy?" It was my first thought. My second stayed on my tongue...James told Roan I looked pretty.

"No, you don't. You never look like a boy, okay? And for future reference, instead of saying something like that, you should take the compliment. Say, 'Thank you.' and lean in for a kiss."

"Oh," I said, pushing the thoughts of James and literally running into him minutes ago to the back burner. Maybe planting a kiss on Roan would make the ache in my heart go away. "Thank you, Roan." I focused on the boy in front of me, grasping his arm with my free hand as I took a step closer. "You're very sweet." I pushed up on my toes and pressed my lips to his.

Was that the right move? The right words?

His hand slid around my waist and pulled me closer.

I'd say that was my answer. Butterflies flitted around in my stomach, and I loved every second of it. Between our lips meeting and the closeness of our bodies, I found it hard to breathe. He really was sweet. I meant that. And I hoped the connection that was developing between us was real. Not the platonic tutor-student relationship.

Moisture clung to my skin from the combination of a hard practice and North Carolina humidity in May. Cayla and I had paired up as the team ran the perimeter of the softball field. We rounded the corner of the outfield on our second lap behind Addison and Summer, heading back toward home plate when Cayla breathed, "Guess who's in the stands?"

My eyes strained to see who it was. Dark hair and a baseball cap could be any number of guys. It was his wide shoulders and chest that made Roan stand out from the others.

"He said he'd give me a ride home after practice." I glanced behind us. Becky and Jaryn were too far behind to hear our conversation. "So what did you think today? Does he like me more than friends? You know I always read guys wrong."

"He was different at lunch," she said. "He met you at your locker, right?"

I nodded.

"I saw him massaging your shoulders while you were in line." She gave me a wink.

I let my mind go back to that moment. His touch felt different from when he checked out my shoulder last week. Shivers trailed down my spine in a good way, like they were doing it now just thinking about it. When he let go and grabbed his food, I wanted to give the lunch lady a dirty look for giving his hands something else to do.

"Yeah, that was different. He's done it before, but not like that—in the middle of a crowded cafeteria." If I had the guts, I'd ask him if this was real, but I didn't want him to stop being my tutor.

She bumped me with her elbow and panted, "He was flirting with you during supper last night."

"How do you know that? You weren't even there."

"Madi texted with me the entire time he was there. For a freshman, she knows how to read a situation. Better than you. No offense."

One more thing Madi was better at than me. "Why do you think she's been...into this? She hasn't made one snide remark about me getting a clue. It's like suddenly she wants us to be buddies, and I'm not sure about it. I mean, she's my sister, and I love her, but..." Madison had always competed against me for everything. I didn't know why, because she didn't even have to try hard to get what she wanted.

Cayla shrugged. "Prom. And maybe she realizes her big sister is graduating soon."

"Great, my little sister feels sorry for me." I hadn't thought about the misery of prom as much the last couple of days. Except when I spilled chocolate gelato down my pantleg after bumping into James. One positive change from prom was that I was looking forward to the end of my high school career. Not knowing what I would do with my life hasn't changed, though.

I sucked in a couple of breaths. "Guess it's better to be friends than enemies."

Cayla's breathing was getting heavy too. "I like her. She's funny. Like you."

I snickered at the thought of my sister being like me. She was more like the best of me and Brendon put together.

"I'm glad you didn't have to deal with James today," she said.

"He was so nice at the dance...until he grabbed my butt when he kissed me. I liked him," I panted. Talking and running two laps after a hard practice may not go together.

"I thought you liked Roan?"

I glanced behind us to make sure no one was near us

before I answered, "I do. I like a lot of guys. They just don't like me."

"That's," Cayla puffed, "not true."

It was true. Which was why I needed a kissing tutor and a boyfriend to prove I wasn't so bad. Would Roan pretend to be my boyfriend?

We pushed through the last stretch and sprinted from third base to home plate. On our walk-out to first, I glanced up at Roan perched on the top of the home stands. A smile stretched across my lips despite trying to catch my breath. His hair curled around the edge of his cap. Even though his eyes were sigh-worthy, he looked good enough to be on the cover of *Elite Athlete* magazine in his sunglasses.

He nodded, lifting one corner of his mouth into a grin.

Giggles from a couple of girls snapped me out of my over-appreciation of my tutor's features. I joined Cayla, Summer, and Addison in the outfield to wait for the rest of the girls so we could do our cooldown.

After we stretched, the team made way for the dugout to get our stuff. I heard Jaryn ask, "What's Roan Martin doing here?"

Becky whispered loud enough I could hear. "He's friends with Tommie."

Jaryn sighed. "He is so hot. I love the tall, dark, and mysterious type."

I lifted my bag on my shoulder and strutted toward Roan, feeling like Wonder Woman. Those cute little underclassmen could drool all they wanted. Roan Martin would be kissing me tonight. I hoped. Even if it was for educational purposes.

13

"It's so hot tonight," I said. "It feels like the middle of July." We crossed the road from visiting Cayla at Masterson's Sporting Goods to Roan's truck. The shower after practice was about to wear off already.

We both slid into his leather seats. At least the tinted windows prevented them from scorching my legs. He started the engine and eased into traffic.

"I heard Charlotte Robinson say something about pier jumping tonight. We could pick Cayla up from work and go," I said. He had been a little on the quiet side tonight. Although, I might have been a tad hypersensitive because I didn't know what the deal was between us. "They'll probably have a fire afterward."

Wait...What was I thinking? My muscles tensed. I didn't do crowds anymore. James and our videoed kiss was the reason I avoided classmates and public locations.

But Roan's tutoring lessons made me forget about all that.

We had a game-free weekend. All we needed to concern ourselves with was fulfilling the contract. It was the only thing I could think about.

His Oakley baseball sunglass lenses were super dark, preventing me from seeing his warm caramel eyes. I couldn't tell what he was thinking.

I cut in before he could agree. "I changed my mind."

"Good. I don't feel like going to the pier," he said as he turned into our subdivision.

Whew. My shoulders fell back in place. "What do you feel like? No parties though," I teased, trying to be as normal as possible. "I'm in charge of you while your grandparents are gone. Remember?"

He flashed me a grin, reached for a pack of mints in his cup holder, and popped a handful in his mouth. "I could kick your butt in Soldier One."

I scoffed. My competitiveness rose up. No matter what, I couldn't let him beat me in my favorite video game. I scoffed and said, "You wish."

He chuckled as we pulled into his garage and parked. He turned the engine off. He said with a chuckle, "I let you win."

"Whatever," I mumbled, stepping out. I shut the door and met him at the entrance of his house.

The garage door powered down as he punched in the

code to unlock the house door. Roan's house was fancier than mine. Mom was always doing some "home improvement" project that lasted for months. I had to admit it was nice when she finished, but Roan's place was always clean and sparkly with fancy furnishings and granite countertops.

He stepped inside and I followed, closing the door behind me.

Roan tossed his keys on the countertop and handed me the roll of mints he brought from the truck. "Want some?" he asked.

Was that a hint a lesson would be in my near future? "Sure." I slipped them from his fingers and crossed the room to the patio door. Looking out over his pool, I popped several mints into my mouth. Why did I order onion rings with my burger earlier? I hoped these things worked. Maybe I should go brush my teeth instead.

I swished the hot cinnamon around my tongue. The more they melted, the spicier they were. I coughed a few times. Just when I thought I had it handled, I coughed more.

"Water," I squeaked, making a dash for the upper cabinet by the sink for a glass. I filled it with tap water and downed half of it.

"You okay?" he asked with laughter from behind me.

In between pants from my tongue being on fire, I nodded and said, "I'm good."

He chuckled. "I should have warned you they were strong." He laced his fingers through mine and tugged me toward the living room. "Come on."

I was glad for the distraction of the firecracker breath mints. They were like an atomic bomb in my mouth. Any trace of onion rings had to be gone after that. We reached the sofa, and he motioned for me to take a seat. We didn't usually sit in this room, especially when his grandparents were gone. My chest tightened as I dropped down in the corner.

Roan sat next to me. Like, really close.

I swallowed and waited for him to say something. It had to be lesson time, right? Not knowing exactly what was going on was torture. My heart rate went from sixty-eight to one-hundred-twenty in 5.0 seconds.

His arm stretched out along the back of the sofa, grazing my shoulders in the process. "Ready for another lesson?"

I nodded, and my throat tightened the same time my belly took a ride. How could I be scared and excited at the same time? It was like bungee jumping off a bridge. The first step would take all the courage I had, but the rush would be worth it.

"I know I said kissing should be spontaneous, but sometimes you know it will happen. You've been worrying too much about what other people think of you." He angled his body closer to mine. "You can't think about other people when you're kissing. It makes it weird." His fingertips stroked down my arm and back up as he taught, leaving a wake of goose bumps. "You just need to be in the moment. It's like when you're pitching, and you're in the zone. All you're focused on is you and the catcher."

"Pitch and catch," I repeated, swallowing my nerves, already focused on his lips. They looked soft. The way they moved when he talked was like an invitation to see if they tasted the same as the cinnamon mints. My hand moved up his arm to the back of his neck.

His breath brushed my lips as he whispered, "Let everything and everyone else fade away, but the sensation."

Our lips met.

I breathed in his sweet and musky amber scent and melted into the heat. My insides wavered between chocolate fondue and over-carbonated soda. Our mouths moved together as if we had done this a thousand times.

If I would have gotten a kissing tutor three years ago, high school could have been a lot more fun. My other hand slid up his chest and wound around his shoulders. The ridge of his muscles under my fingers triggered more fizzy bubbles. Was it normal to want more?

Roan's arms brought me closer, but not for long. He ended our kiss, pressing his forehead to mine. "Whoa," he uttered with his eyes still closed.

"Was that good?" I asked, breathing as if I'd taken a lap around the field.

A huge grin spread across his face when he chuckled. His eyelids slid closed. "That was good," he said with a raspy voice.

He was right. Letting everything else fade away was amazing—addictive. I was floating, and buzzing, and a few giggles bounced around my ribcage. I wanted more. "Maybe we should practice. Work on the next lesson." I didn't want to stop kissing. Like, ever.

His eyes popped open, and he put some space between us. "Maybe we should take a break."

I asked, "Practice makes perfect, doesn't it?" I gave him my best flirty smile. Which was probably ridiculous, since it had never, in my entire life, worked on any of the guys I had used it on.

His eyebrows squished together. He asked, "What was that?"

I puffed out a deflated breath, folded my arms, and sunk back into the leather cushion of the sofa. "That was supposed to be my flirty smile." I gave him the truth. It was still my best friend in front of me.

He chuckled, shaking his head. "Please, never do that again. You've got a great smile. You don't need to do something fake." He leaned across and placed a kiss on my pouty lips.

It caught me off guard. Was that part of the "tutoring?" I didn't think it was.

His eyes widened when he realized what he'd done, and he straightened, moving back into his own space.

My heart pounded. I wanted to admit that I liked him kissing me. Him. Not my tutor. It might be a line we shouldn't cross as friends, but I didn't want to lose the amazingness that had sparked between us either.

Before I could get any words out, he stood and headed away from me and toward the upstairs. "Loser makes a protein shake," he called over his shoulder.

Nice, Tommie. I grunted out of frustration. *He doesn't see you like that. No boy sees you like that. When are you going to get a clue?*

14

My phone dinged. I checked the message and then shut it off. "Cayla's here," I said to Juju. Since I didn't respond to her messages earlier, she sent one to Madi that she was coming over. Cayla was the only person I didn't mind being around right now. I rubbed Juju's belly with my foot and wiped my hands on the kitchen towel. "Let's go unlock the door."

She whined and lie back down on the rug. I left her behind, crossing through the mess Mom called a "work in progress" to the front door to open it. "Hey," I greeted in a less than chipper tone.

"That bad?" she asked, shutting the door behind her and following me back to the kitchen.

When I made it back to the stove, I flipped the bacon I had cooking in the oven and put the pan back in for a few more minutes.

"Oh, my gosh," Cayla said, taking a seat at the bar. "Giant chocolate chip pancakes, maple syrup, chocolate syrup, whipped cream with bacon on top? Girl, what happened?"

I sighed, moving the pancakes to a plate. "I already told you everything when I got home last night."

"Where's Madi?"

"She's out jogging on the beach, keeping her perfect little body looking..." The chunk of butter I dropped on the griddle sizzled. "Perfect."

"Tommie, she's not perfect. No one is perfect. She's been in your corner, remember?"

My mouth watered from the melting butter aroma. I was seriously considering taking a bite of what was left from the stick. If I'd been alone, I might have. Instead, I ladled the batter into two giant mounds, sprinkling chocolate chips on top each one.

Madi had been nicer since the whole kissing tutor idea. I was still trying to figure out why. Now that I thought about it, she had cut back about the time James asked me to prom. I sighed thinking about how boys liked her, and she didn't need a kissing tutor. Ugh. It wasn't her fault Roan took the job no one wanted, and I wanted him to like kissing me...want me as a girlfriend. "Yeah. It's just...I'm starting to like him, like him. You know? But kissing me has no effect on him. He doesn't seem fazed at all. It's like he's tutoring me in calculus. I don't know if I should keep doing this. I already felt like a loser, and this is making it worse."

"If he wasn't such a bear, I'd say he was on the top five list of hotties at school," she said. "But I think you're immune to his grumpiness, so why not go for it?" Cayla went to the fridge and brought the milk back to the island, pouring herself a glass.

"He is top five. He is not a bear. And obviously, he doesn't see me like that. At all." I wasn't sure anyone did. An invisible hand wrapped its fingers around my heart and squeezed. Was it possible to have a heartbreak without being involved in a relationship?

"He's definitely attracted to you or he wouldn't want to kiss you. And he said your kisses were, 'wow' last night. Right?" She gave me a broad, toothy grin, wiggling her eyebrows up and down.

It made me chuckle. Which was good, because the doubt consuming my brain and pain in my heart sucked. "He said, 'Whoa.' And that it was good. But that doesn't mean he wants to kiss me when he's not being the tutor." I flipped the cakes and pulled the bacon out of the oven, setting it on a trivet.

Food wasn't always my go-to when I was sad or upset. I just knew I needed to get out of bed this morning or I would end up staying in my room all day. Chocolate chip pancakes were never a bad idea.

After the cakes were done, I shut off the burners and

piled food on top of my plate. Cayla did the same, maybe a ton less excessive than me.

"Let's eat on the patio," I said. "I think I could use some sunshine." Sunshine cured a lot of things. So did endorphins. Maybe I should have gone with Madi. She asked me to. The sound of ocean waves rolling in and crashing on the beach had a way of mending things too.

Cayla shoved her phone in her pocket from the countertop. It dinged twice, but she didn't bother checking it.

We stacked our plates, forks, napkins, and drinks on a big tray and carried it out the backdoor to the patio. This was one place Mom had finished. And though the backyard wasn't that big, she had made it comfy.

"The gardenias smell amazing" Cayla said as she sat down at the table.

I breathed in deep. "Yeah, it's nice out here."

"Dad hates messing with flower beds and landscaping. He wants to mow it all," she said, waving a hand toward the flowers lining the outer steps of the patio.

I cut my first bite and stuck it in my mouth. "Mmm," I moaned, closing my eyes for a moment to savor the sweet reward of my cooking efforts.

We ate in silence for a few minutes. Cayla was probably giving me space without letting me be alone. It didn't take long for Roan to fill my thoughts again. I asked, "What if this makes things weird and ruins our friendship?"

"You guys have been friends a long time. It's worth finding out," she said. "You're the yin to his yang."

I rolled my eyes at that craziness.

She giggled and asked, "What?" Cayla's phone dinged again. She took another bite of food and lowered her fork to check it. With her mouth full, she said, "These are amazing, by the way."

She scrolled through her screen and gasped. "Guess what?"

I devoured half of my food in the time it took her to read all her messages. "What?" I replied with my mouth full.

The back door squeaked shut as Madi came out of the house with a plate full of breakfast. "Tommie," Madi said. "I know you're in a bad mood, but this breakfast smells so good. Thanks for cooking." She sat down across from me.

"Sure," I deadpanned. At least I wasn't eating by myself. That would be extra pathetic.

Cayla let out a high-pitched squeal.

I flinched, squeezing my eyes shut until it was over, asking, "What's the deal?"

Cayla squealed again and said, "The baseball team invited us to go to Sweet Water Falls."

"Really?" Madi wiggled her eyebrows at me.

"You can go in my place, Mads. I don't feel like it. Especially after eating two plate-sized pancakes with chocolate sauce and about two pounds of bacon." My belly pooched over my sleep shorts. I rubbed it and said, "Me in a swimsuit would not be attractive." As if it ever was.

"You can't be serious," Cayla griped, her lips pressed into a thin line.

Madi asked, "Is Roan going?"

I shrugged. If he was going, I didn't want to be there.

"Hey," Roan's voice called through the fence. "Let me in."

I eyed Madi, silently telling her to do it. Our fence didn't have a gate, and it was too tall to climb over.

"I'll meet you there," she called to Roan, standing and heading back in the house.

Cayla winked and whispered, "He wants you to go."

I shook my head. "I'm not sure I can do this, Cayla. Kiss him and pretend I don't feel something. It's making me feel worse."

She wiped a drop of chocolate sauce off of her chin. Her lips curved into a gentle smile. "How do you know he's not feeling the same thing?"

Because I was Tommie the tomboy. My throat tightened. I drank down the rest of my milk, hoping it would go away. It didn't. I stared at the gray clouds dotting the blue skies for a minute, but the tears still threatened. "I think I'm going to take a shower. Let me know when he's gone."

"I think he likes you," Cayla said, watching me move to the door.

I shook my head but didn't look back before I turned the knob and walked into the kitchen, leaving the door open for Madi. She passed by me with a smile.

Roan stood next to the food with a plate in hand. He forked a pancake and said, "I sent you some messages. You never responded."

I shrugged, rinsed my dishes, and put them in the dishwasher. "My phone's shut off."

He gave me a look as if he couldn't understand why I would do such a thing.

Of course, he wouldn't. He's a guy. Mom told me once that guys put all their thoughts and emotions in little boxes. They liked things to stay separate. Women connected everything together. Which was why us kissing means nothing to him and had me in a state of confusion and turmoil.

"I need a shower," I mumbled and headed out of the room. We were close friends, but he's not a mind reader. Though he had done quite a lot of that over the years.

"Where's your mom?" he asked.

Where she always was. I called back over my shoulder, "Work," and continued to the stairwell. Juju came alongside me, and we climbed the steps together toward my room.

Even after chocolate chip pancakes gloom continued

to cloud my mood. If sun, chocolate, and bacon couldn't reverse my sulking, music was worth a try. I scrolled through my playlists until I found a good dance one and connected my phone to the speaker.

While it played, I moved my body to the rhythm and rummaged through my dresser for some clothes. My sister's "garbage sack" comment came to mind. "So what if Roan doesn't want to kiss me for real, Juju girl? I still need to start dressing better, right?"

She whined and laid her head on her paws.

It was possible I had other kinds of shorts in my drawer. I searched through one stack and started on the other when I heard a knock.

I turned and saw Roan leaning against the door frame with his hands stuffed in his shorts pockets. Gorgeous liquid gold eyes, warm tanned skin, thick dark hair. Ugh.

What was he doing up here? Did he hear me talking to Juju? I raised my eyebrows, "Yeah?"

"Are you mad at me?" he asked, striding into my room until we were inches apart.

My chest tightened. Why did he have to look so kissable all the time? This was the reason I shouldn't have agreed to him tutoring me. Itwas causing a rift between us already. And for what? I was still just a buddy. That's all I would ever be. To anyone. I shook my head and looked down at Juju. "It's me." Even as I said it, I could feel the moisture threatening to pool in my eyes.

He chuckled. "Are you using the 'It's not you, it's me' line?"

A hint of a smile inched halfway across my face. Maybe I used that line, but I just wanted him to go away so I could wallow in my self-pity for the morning. Okay, maybe for the weekend, but then I'd be over Roan and move on with my un-kiss-able, un-date-able reputation. I swallowed, keeping my eyes down, and said, "I'm not sure the tutoring thing is working out."

He inched closer. "What are you talking about? You've only had a couple of lessons, and you're doing great."

I took a step back, watching my toes as they dug into the carpet. He wouldn't get the whole truth but enough he would ease up with the questions. I met his gaze and said, "Look, you're my best friend, and I don't want to lose that."

He tilted his head, his deep-set caramel eyes softening the wall I tried to build. "We're not going to."

I looked up at the ceiling. The tightness in my chest increased. "You were right, okay? It was a dumb idea. I'm not good at this." I turned away and grabbed the first pair of shorts I saw and closed the drawer. "Besides, guys just don't see me as potential girlfriend material. Or a girl." I mumbled the last part under my breath. I turned back, folded my arms across my chest, and said, "Maybe college will be different."

He closed the distance I had put between us. "It's not entirely dumb." He chuckled. "I'm actually having fun."

"Great. I'm glad you're having a good laugh on me." Ugh, my heart dove over the line last night, and now he was making fun of me? My eyes stung, but I fought it.

"A bunch of the guys are going to the Falls today. Come with me." He reached out and clasped my hands in his.

I peered up through my lashes at his wide grin. "Go with you as friends?" It slipped out. I didn't mean to say that out loud.

He cocked his head to the side, looking at me as if he were solving a riddle. "Yeah," he said in a way that sounded like a question.

"I don't know. I need to clean," I rushed out while the pancakes hardened in my belly. Ugh. I only needed to clean up the kitchen and my room, but he didn't know that.

"Come on," he drawled, changing his expression to a grin as he slid his hand around my waist. He began moving with the beat of the music. Roan's dad was involved in competitive ballroom dancing when he was in his teens in Argentina. Roan took lessons when he was younger.

He taught me to dance a few years ago but made me promise not to tell anyone he took lessons. If his teammates knew, they'd never let him live it down.

But I didn't want to dance. Not when the sting of his rejection from last night was still raw. One long kiss and that was it. We were all alone at his house for hours and he didn't want to practice kissing.

He twirled me away, stepping close behind me. I ended up with my arms around my middle and my back against his chest.

"It'll be fun," he said. "Bring Cayla and Madi, if you want."

And there it was. He only meant for me to come along as his buddy. The sparks I felt, the attraction, it was one-sided. My side. Totally unrequited... as usual.

He moved our hips to the beat of a song. His voice dropped low as he said, "You were right last night. We should've kept practicing."

Why would he use that smooth, sexy voice, say those words, dance this close? It was torture. Being this close made my body think what was going on was real, real chemistry.

If I admitted I was falling for him, would it ruin our friendship? Would I ruin it by keeping it to myself? I had to ask, "Can I ask you something?"

"Ask away," he said, his cheek pressing against my hair.

Facing away from him would make it a thousand times easier—I hoped. "Promise you'll tell me the truth?"

He slowed to a sway and answered, "Promise."

My mouth went dry, and I tried to swallow but couldn't. Even my breathing had quickened. "When you, we...I'm..." How could I say this without him or me freaking out? "Am I just the entertainment here?"

We stopped moving but he said nothing. He fit around me like a cocoon, and it was everything I wanted and was afraid I wouldn't have.

His head shook against mine. "No."

I swallowed my nerves and asked another question. "Would it be too weird if I said I like kissing you?"

He lowered his lips close to my ear and whispered, "I like it too."

I sucked in a quick breath. I thought my tight muscles would release after he agreed, but my body became even more excited. "Really?" I asked. "What do we do?"

"I don't know," he said, pausing for a moment. "Keep doing what we've been doing the last few days."

I nodded, relieved he didn't say he's the tutor, and that's it. Excited the sparks and electricity buzzing inside my body wasn't only me.

His cheek pressed against the side of my hair I had piled up on top of my head. "You smell like pancakes." He chuckled. "And bacon."

That was exactly what ten-year-old Roan would have said. It kind of ruined the moment. "Gee, thanks." I tried to pull away, but he twirled me back around to face him.

"We might need to practice what you've learned so far." He grinned, causing my stomach to quiver as he dipped his mouth closer to mine.

I leaned away. "Whoa!"

Roan came closer.

I squirmed out of his hold. It wasn't a given, but lesson three could happen and that might have involved our tongues doing the tango. Since that would be a first for me, I definitely wanted it to be a good experience. "I need to brush my teeth. Please," I said.

He held his hands up, stepping back toward my door. "If that's the way you want it. Guess I'll be downstairs." His wide smile, the way it hitched higher on one side than the other, almost made me change my mind. But a quick flashback to my first kiss was enough to wait.

That, and the appearance of my brother behind Roan. "What's going on?" Brendan asked.

Roan jumped, giving my brother a playful shove, and grumbled, "Dude."

Brendan chuckled, clamping down on Roan's shoulders, and then released him.

Roan shook his head and said, "I'm about to clean up breakfast. You want some?"

"No thanks," Brendan said. "I just came back to get my wetsuit. A storm's coming."

I folded my arms across my chest and asked, "You're going out in a storm?"

He turned, headed for his room, and called back, "Nope. Going out before the storm gets here."

I met Roan in the hall. He pointed his thumb behind him as he walked backward toward the stairs, trying to control his smile. "We'll, um...I'll go eat."

I nodded and escaped to the bathroom, turning the shower on. Did that just happen? What was that anyway? I thought I had asked if he liked me, but now I was even more confused.

15

"Looking good, Martin!" I whooped for Roan after he'd hit a continuous ten for ten. Again.

My brother was right. A storm came in and the trip to Sweet Water Falls didn't happen. Cayla, Roan, and I decided to go to Home Run Park and have some fun in the batting cages.

She just left to go make some money since it rained. Her disappointment from not getting to watch "bare-chested baseball players frolicking through the waterfall" had her "depressed." That was the word she used, anyway.

A few of the baseball guys had trickled in while Roan was in the batting cage and took residence in another cage not far away.

Batting practice was what we needed anyway. If we

each got another win next week, both teams would go to playoffs.

Roan pulled his helmet off, wearing a huge grin, and opened the cage door. His hair stuck up on one side. I thought about fixing it but decided I liked the boyish look on him. "Man, that felt good. This is the best I've hit in weeks."

I raised my hand to bump against his. "Your form was masterful," I said.

His wide eyes danced as he leaned closer and said, "Masterful? I like it." He gripped my waist, and warmth spidered around the contact. "Let's see the replay." He removed his grip, draping his arm on my shoulder instead.

I brought up the first video and pressed play. Watching yourself on video was a good way to see what you were doing right or wrong.

"Okay. My turn." I slipped on my helmet and gripped my bat.

Roan put his helmet and bat in my bag. He readied his camera phone as I stepped up to the plate.

"Ready?" I asked.

He nodded, and I pressed the button to engage the pitching machine. After a couple of adjustments, it was at the right strike zone for my height.

I had two hits right off.

Roan moved a little closer with his phone, videotaping my swing. "What do you say we get some tutoring practice in tonight?" he asked right as the ball released from the machine.

I missed. Just him talking about kissing threw my swing off.

He laughed, but I ignored him, readying myself for the next ball. He mused about where our next lesson would be, and I fouled the pitch off.

"That counts as a miss," he said.

"No way!" I laughed, waiting for the machine. "The bat hit the ball."

I hit the next ball despite his chatter.

"Aw, you're blushing," he teased.

When my ten were up, I met Roan off to the side to watch the videos of my form. "Eight out of ten isn't bad," I said.

"I beat you," he teased.

I elbowed him. We both hated to lose. I defended myself. "Only because you distracted me."

He chuckled and teased me some more. "I never knew talking about lessons and tutoring would make you so nervous. I exposed your Kryptonite."

"Shut up and play the next video," I said but didn't dare look him in the eye. My face was on fire, knowing that he knew kissing him made me nervous. His teasing seemed like flirting, but I failed in that department, so I had to wait and see what happened. If I didn't restrain myself, tackling him and kissing him first.

"I think the rain stopped. Let's go say hi to Logan and the guys," he said, nodding to the players a few cages down from ours. "Then we can go get something to eat."

I groaned inside. The guys wouldn't say anything in front of Roan, but I still felt awkward around them. "You go ahead. I'm going to the bathroom and then we can go," I said. I glanced at the guys. "I don't really want to hang out over there, if you don't mind."

He worked his jaw to the side. "You can't avoid them forever. They used to be your friends too," he said.

I shrugged and turned away to slide my helmet and bat into my bag. I lifted the strap to my shoulder and said, "I'll take my time."

He pushed open the cage door and let me go through first, gripping my ponytail as I stepped by. He swung it over the top of my head, and it whacked me in the face. It was his way of easing any tension from what he had said.

"Hey," I yelped. I turned and swatted at his arm.

He chuckled. "I'll be ready as soon as you get back."

I traveled down the path between the cages but tried not to be seen looking at anyone. Summer and Gabe stood at the plate in the last cage. His arms were around her, gripping the bat with his fingers on top of hers. It was so sweet, and fun, and flirty.

The thought of Roan snuggling up behind me

pushed my heart off rhythm. Summer's giggles filled the air as I passed by. Her super light blonde hair and bright blue eyes made her stand out—stunning. But she didn't have curves. Her figure resembled a boy's more than mine. Gabe obviously liked her shape though, or he would have put at least an inch of space between them.

I made a left into the bathroom and took my time. There was no way I could handle standing around with the baseball guys. Not anymore. Pre-prom, it wouldn't have been an issue.

Roan was right. I couldn't hide away forever. Maybe I could do it if he was beside me as my boyfriend.

After I used the bathroom and washed up, I sent Cayla a message.

Tommie: Great job in the cages today. We're gonna kick the Panther's butts!
Cayla: Thanks!
Tommie: We're about to leave. Have fun at work.
Cayla: Mr. McHottie just walked in. Excuse me while I drool.

That girl was as bad as me. Except she was cute and petite compared to my fierceness. Guess that's why she got her own date to prom and I had to beg my friends for help.

I shoved the phone in my pocket and looked in the

mirror. At least I didn't wear my "garbage bag" shorts. We were done batting. I didn't need to be fierce now, so I pulled the rubber band out of my ponytail and combed my fingers through my dirty blonde strands.

Maybe I should start wearing eyeliner all the time. And carrying lip gloss with me. I shrugged at myself. It was as good as I got without help from my sister.

I hitched my bag over my shoulder and headed back out. Roan had enough time hanging with his teammates. Summer and Gabe were just as adorable as I strode back through. Instead of wishing I had something I didn't, I focused ahead on Roan with his arms stretched high, gripping the wire cage with his fingers. A wide strip of bare skin between his shirt hem and his shorts drew my gaze. He made the other guys look like skinny weaklings.

I heard a bat crack and caught the end of Logan's swing. James wasn't anywhere around. Which was odd because when it came to baseball, he and Logan were inseparable.

Roan glanced over and saw me approaching. He dropped his arm, and one corner of his mouth tugged up, and then the other. It warmed my insides. He jogged to meet me and we exited the building without a word.

After the door closed behind us, thunder cracked. I searched the clouds above for lightning but saw nothing. "Thanks for not making a big deal about me talking to the guys."

"Anything for you, Toms," he joked. "It was good to leave on a ten for ten. Plus, I beat you, so..." He bumped my shoulder.

Thunder rolled through the clouds again. I shook my head and muttered, "Whatever."

Rain pelted the edge of the parking lot, heading our direction. "We might get wet," he said.

"Maybe you shouldn't have parked in no-man's-land," I teased. He always did that if it were possible. The truck was his baby. His grandparents gave it to him as a sixteenth birthday gift.

We picked up our pace. "Should we make a run for it?" he asked.

All of a sudden, the rain poured down on top of us. We sprinted to the last row of the parking lot. Laughter rolled out of me. Running was pointless. The downpour soaked us from our heads to our shoes.

I reached for Roan's arm. "Your seats. They'll be ruined," I teased.

"That's why I got leather," he said, grinning.

It wasn't funny, but laughter spilled out of me. I felt like a kid playing, running down the beach in the rain. I let go of his arm and jumped on his back, wrapping my arms around his wet shirt. I planted a giggly kiss on his cheek. My insides warmed.

He gripped my legs, putting us in motion, and said, "We should play in the rain more often."

I pressed my cheek to his as water streamed down our faces. "We should," I agreed.

We laughed and joked the entire trek. By the time we got to the truck, the rain had let up to a sprinkle. He opened the passenger back door for me to put my bag on the floorboard and shut it.

The matted mess of my hair clung to my cheeks. I was breathless from giggling and being that close to him. Even though I had jumped on his back a ton of times over the years, it was different—everything was different between us. I gathered my hair to the side and wrung the water out.

I caught a glimpse of Roan taking his shirt off. "Good idea," he said, wringing the water from it before tossing it by my bag and closing the door.

My eyes scanned his arms, chest, abs. A smirk tugged at his lips as he watched me watching him.

Busted.

My heart whirled in my chest as I dropped my gaze to the wet pavement. I wrung my hair again just to pretend I was doing something. "Gah, I probably look like a total mess," I said. I reached for the front handle, but his hand covered mine, tugging it away.

"I like it," he said in a low voice. "You look like...fun."

I peered up at him, trying to figure out exactly what he was doing, what he meant. Was he teasing? His eyes glowed like liquid gold. It was a smolder that made my insides hum. I couldn't look away. Not that I wanted to.

He laced our fingers together and backed me against the truck.

My heart raced, warming my body while his other hand gripped my waist. Fizzy bubbles erupted and danced in my stomach. This boy was officially, definitely, more to me than a friend.

As he dipped his mouth to mine, my breath caught. When our lips met, heat sparked in my core. I untangled our fingers and slid my hands around his wet physique and up his back, melding our bodies together. Not that I knew what I was doing. I went with it, doing my best to be in the moment like he taught me.

His fingers grazed the bare skin of my neck, sliding under my hair. To look at Roan, it was obvious that he was strong, but the way he held and kissed me was a different kind of strong. The kind that says, *I got you—you can trust me no matter what.*

Could this be something real? Even if it wasn't, I didn't want to let go of the way my heartbeat pulsed through my veins or the weightlessness of being in his arms. When I was kissing him, I wasn't one of the boys.

He pulled away enough to confess, "I wanted to do that since we got here."

"Me too," I breathed. I tilted my head so I could kiss his neck below his ear.

As soon as my lips touched the wetness on his skin, a gruff breath whooshed out of him. His cheek brushed mine, and his lips moved along my jawline. They were feather-light as they traced to my neck. Goosebumps from his warm breath spread across my skin, and I shivered.

He groaned. "We should get out of here." His lips found mine for a hurried kiss. "Let's go warm up in the hot tub." The handle clicked as Roan twirled me around. I ended up standing in front of the open door, awaiting to climb in.

16

Best friends status meant I kept a swimsuit and extra clothes at Roan's house. His grandma suggested it years ago since I was over there all the time. I slipped on the suit in the bathroom and combed the tangled mess on top of my head.

My hair did look as bad as I thought. Why Roan said otherwise was beyond me. But the whole quiet drive to his house, I wondered if he regretted everything from this morning, flirting in the cages, and that amazing make-out session by his truck. It probably wasn't officially making-out, but it was the closest I had ever been.

Roan's arms stretched along the back of the hot tub. His hair had grown shaggy, but I liked it. I opened the patio door and slid it closed behind me, crossing the concrete to join him. *Act normal, Tommie. Everything is fine.*

After I sat my phone by the towel and lifted myself onto the corner, I swiveled my body around. Being five-ten meant my legs were long enough to sit on the edge without using the steps. I dipped my toes under the surface until they rested on the seat. "Ah." I sighed.

When we walked inside and the air conditioning met my chilled body, it got worse. I sank all the way into the steamy water until it covered my shoulders.

Music played from his outdoor speakers. I closed my eyes and tried to forget about the crazy mess swirling in my head. The jets did their job of kneading the muscles that had tensed from getting chilled.

"Toms?" Roan said in a soft tone. His fingers slid over my hand and laced with mine.

My body relaxed a bit more at his touch. I opened my eyes, rolling my head against the wall of the tub to meet his gaze. The emotional rollercoaster I'd been on for the last week had me wondering if I should end the contract with the kissing tutor.

"I messed up," he said, searching my eyes. He had a tiny crease between his eyebrows.

I didn't know what he was looking for. My stomach tightened as I waited for him to explain.

"It should have been me who took you to prom," he said. "We both would have had a much better time."

A flicker of warmth sparked in my chest. "I didn't

think you'd want to go with a friend your senior year. Did you want to ask me?"

He shrugged. "I think so. I mean," he let out a growl, "I hated every minute of suggesting to James to ask you. And then the stupid video." He shook his head. "We ended up together that night anyway, watching movies on your laptop." He grinned, squeezing my hand.

Movies with Roan was sweet. He let me cry and snot on him, but most of all, he didn't let me out of his arms all night. Dad gave the best hugs, and I missed that. Roan was always there to pick up the pieces.

Wait, he wanted to take me? "You wanted to go to prom with me? Like, as a date?" I asked.

He held his grin in place. "It was on my mind. I wasn't sure what was happening between us, if anything. I wasn't sure if you felt the same way because you wanted a 'real date' to your senior prom."

My mouth dropped open. One decision could have changed my life. I would've never had to deal with all the humiliation if Roan would've asked me to prom. The question was, would I have gone?

We'd gone to pretty much every dance, but only as friends, buddies. He could have been my first kiss. Ugh, I wish it would have been him. I groaned. "Look where that got me." My mind raced. Would I have wanted to be his date? "Honestly, I don't know what I would have said then. But I'm glad I came to you with my crazy kissing tutor idea."

"Me too," he said, grinning. I loved those full lips.

"Are you going to hold my hand like this at school?" Talking about this, us, had my nerves tightening in my chest at first. Now that I knew he wanted to take me to prom as a date, I wanted to know everything.

"I don't know," he said. "I haven't thought about it."

"Do you think about anything other than baseball or food?" I teased. Knowing the connection between us was real, more than friends, had me floating.

He settled back against the tub and closed his eyes, keeping our hands together. "Sure. This song makes me think of you."

I couldn't believe what was happening to me. The signals weren't mixed up. Instead of asking a ton of questions about him and me and us, I relaxed and listened to the lyrics. Any boy thinking about me when they heard this song would be a thrill. But Roan Martin, my friend, the only guy I could count on thinking of me that way, made it so much sweeter.

Song after song played while we held hands amid unspoken bliss. My favorite song filled the air and my body. I automatically moved with the rhythm. It wasn't exactly slow but would be perfect dancing with a guy who was totally into me. I closed my eyes and imagined dancing with Roan. I sighed. "I love this song."

"I know," he said in a warm voice that made me want to read his expression.

I opened my eyes and set my gaze on him. The sweet, dopey smile on his face stirred up the fizzy bubbles in my chest.

His fingers grazed my waist as he slid closer to me. "I want you to think of me every time you hear it." He pressed his lips against mine.

That was the dreamiest thing he had ever said. I moved my mouth with his. A hint of mint lingered on his breath. I tasted his lips to see if the mint was there, and wow, my bold move was worth it.

The warmth of his tongue moving across my lips caused the tiny fizzy bubbles to explode one by one like popcorn in my chest. We explored this new way of kissing for the rest of the song.

When the song ended, I was on his lap. I didn't know if I moved me or he moved me. All I knew was, "This feels good." I didn't mean to say it out loud, but it was out there, and I didn't care. I didn't worry about what he would say or think. Not at the moment anyway.

He buried his face in my shoulder and tightened his grip until we couldn't get any closer. "Yeah." His chest expanded against mine.

It was a good thing I used mouthwash while I was changing.

I cleared my throat and said exactly what I thought,

"The taste of your lips will be the only thing I can think about when I hear that song now."

His body shook with laughter. "That's freaking awesome." He pressed his forehead against mine, kissing the tip of my nose. "This could be so good, Toms. You know? You and me."

"I think so too." I'd been wasting my time all year trying to find a boy who liked me. And though I thought my connection to Roan was changing, I wanted a boyfriend, a close connection with a guy. As long as they saw me as a girl, preferably a girlfriend.

But this, with Roan, was so much better than I could have imagined.

"I'm starving." He leaned back. "Who's cooking at your house tonight?"

"Not me. Mom worked the day shift, so she might. You want me to check?" I asked.

He loosened his grip. "Yeah."

I shifted off of his lap and crossed the tub. I dried my hands on the towel next to my phone and sent my sister a message.

Tommie: What's for supper?

Madi: Mom's working on the house. Pizza or Chinese?

"Ugh," I groaned. "Mom's working on the house tonight."

"Good, I'll help," Roan said. "I like hanging out with your family."

I rolled my eyes and turned back to him. "What about this?" I motioned between us. "We can't be like this around Mom or she might get weird. She might not let you come up to my room or let us be alone at your house."

He tilted his head, tapping a finger at his temple. "Hm. What if..." He crossed the tub, placed his hands on either side of me, and murmured, "We eat there and then watch a movie later?"

I grinned, loving the way his actions caused my stomach to dip in reaction. "The theater or here?" I gave in to wanting to touch him and let my fingers grip his waist, bringing us closer.

"Either." His eyes darted back and forth between my eyes and mouth. I stayed focused on his soft golden heaven until our lips met again. This time I was the one who slid my tongue along his lips. His mouth parted and his warm tongue met mine and tangled in a give and take that set me on fire. We were late to dinner, but it was worth it. And I couldn't wait for more later.

Kissing Roan got better every time.

17

Roan and I followed the line of players waiting to board the bus. "I wish we could sit together," I said.

"Coach knows what he's doing, keeping us separated. We need to focus on the game if we want to make playoffs." He leaned down and whispered, "Besides, I'm still reeling from when you attacked me this morning."

Heat touched my cheeks, thinking about the way he kissed me before school, and I gave him a heavy nudge.

He stumbled off balance, chuckling.

"I don't remember it happening quite like that," I said with a grin, thinking about this morning and yesterday and Saturday's kisses. My fingers grazed his, but he moved his hand to grip the strap of his bag.

My eyebrows squished together. Did he not want to hold my hand?

He glanced around and asked, "Oh, it did. How about a repeat when we get back?"

He probably thought I just bumped his hand instead of wanting to feel his warmth. He was flirting with me. I think. "Maybe," I said in a coy tone. At least that's what I was going for.

The freshman boy in front of me climbed the steps. I knew every varsity player, but I didn't keep up with the underclassman unless they had some talent. Roan poked me in the back until I took the first step. I climbed the rest and dropped my bag with the others.

Cayla had secured us a seat a halfway back and I slid in next to her. "Hey," I said.

My eyes trailed Roan as he passed by. My smile fell when he didn't even glance in my direction. I faced forward, confusion plaguing me again.

Cayla tugged the chords of her earbuds until they popped out. "What's wrong?"

I shook my head. "It's probably nothing. I'll tell you after we get moving."

"Okay," she said. She stuck in one earbud and scrolled to her softball road trip playlist. We always listened to her playlist or watched videos together to and from our away games.

Summer and Addison settled in the seat ahead of us. The color of their hair was close to polar opposites. I had never seen anyone with hair as light as Summer's. She had it in her usual braid for catching.

The bus driver closed the door and eased us out of the parking lot. When we reached the highway, Addison craned her neck and asked us, "You guys ready? This game is ours."

Cayla agreed, "We own the Tigers."

I nodded. "I'm ready," I said, though I wasn't entirely sure that was true.

Summer raised her fist over her head so I could bump it and said, "You've got this, Jenkins."

After we were on our way, Cayla scooted across the seat until our shoulders touched. "What's up?"

I sunk down in the seat and let it out. "When we're at church or school, Roan acts like we're the same as we always have been. I tried to hold his hand while we waited to get on the bus, but he moved his. And he said it was a good thing that we couldn't sit by each other because we need to 'focus.'" I reached back and pulled my ponytail over my shoulder, running my fingers through it. "Do you think he's embarrassed to be seen with me like that?"

She shrugged. "We need to win this game today. If you were sitting together, the game wouldn't even be on your mind. And—" she bumped me with her elbow— "who would I sit with?"

"I guess," I said, not quite believing it was nothing.

"And he probably didn't know you were trying to hold his hand." She tilted her head down, eyebrows arched high on her forehead. "We are talking about Roan here."

I giggled. Cayla made Roan out to be a Neanderthal. He was a smart guy though. They just didn't always see eye to eye on things. "Did you see him walk by? He didn't even look at me."

"Oh, my gosh, girl. Don't go all possessive girlfriend," she grumbled, shaking her head. "You're worried about nothing."

I sucked in a deep breath and blew it out. Questions ran through me. It didn't feel right, but I had been wrong about reading guys forever. I didn't want to be that kind of girlfriend. "I definitely don't want to go there."

Cayla held her hand out for the plug of my headphones. "Now, let's get in the zone."

I unwrapped the headphone chord from my phone and handed it to her. She took the end, pushed it into the dual headphone plug adapter, and tunes played through it. We hunkered down and went through our routine of music and videos and getting our mindset on winning.

Only I couldn't stop daydreaming about what Roan said while we were in the hot tub Saturday...or my first tongue-tangled kiss.

Cayla checked her phone as I trudged from the bus to Roan's truck. "Ugh. Dad said he needs me to close up at the store. Can you believe that? I just got back from a game. I'm gross and in my uniform."

I sighed. The weight from being benched still sat heavy on my chest. At least Mazzie pulled out a win. "Sorry you have to go in."

She gave me a side hug and asked, "You going to be okay?"

"Yeah," I said, though I wasn't sure.

"Okay. I need to hurry. Talk later," she called as she jogged to her Jeep.

The softball team had already passed me, and even some of the baseball team, I was going so slow. I didn't feel like moving faster.

Roan caught up with me as soon as Cayla got in her Jeep. He stretched his arm across my shoulders and pulled me close. "Don't let London get to you. She's a spoiled wannabe. You're better than this, Toms. You're the best pitcher around. And after playoffs, you'll get recruited to one of the colleges that were too dumb the first go-around."

I slid my arm around his waist, needing his comfort. He didn't pull away from me this time. London made a joke about me being a man-eater on the drive to the game and got a big laugh from at least half of the players. Which set me off in the wrong direction. She started up again during warmups while Violet Russell was catching her. Making kissing noises during my wind-up, calling me guppy girl, anything she could think of. I let her get in my head. Again. Coach benched me during the fourth inning. "Thanks for believing in me."

"It's true," he said. "Now get your head screwed on right."

"Yes, Catch," I said and leaned my head on his shoulder. One breath made me think better of it though, and I straightened. A few inches closer to his armpit made a huge difference.

Catchers wore a mask, chest protector, shin guards, and their mitt was heavier. Which meant they got hot under all that. A lot sweatier than the rest of the players.

"What's the matter, I stink too bad for you?" he asked.

"No more than usual, I guess," I deadpanned.

He looped the crook of his arm around my neck and pulled my face even closer to his pit. Laughing the whole time, of course.

We bounced onto the gravel parking lot, and I shoved against his abs, but it was no use. He held me firmly against him. "Stop! Ugh, you're disgusting!"

He loosened his grip and said, "You're such a weakling."

"Ew, you're so rank." I elbowed him in the side.

He leaned over and kissed my cheek. "You still smell like vanilla."

It was probably because I sat on the bench for over half the game and didn't break a sweat. Since his comment was accompanied with a kiss, I think it was a compliment.

We dropped our bags in the bed of his truck and got in. He started the engine as I leaned over the console.

"Thanks for the pep talk," I said and planted a kiss on his cheek. He was right. I was tougher than London's words. I used to have ice in my veins when I pitched. Any chatter the other team threw at me bounced off my invisible shield. It was a little tougher when it came from your own teammate though.

He flashed me a grin. "Anything for you, Toms."

I buckled my seatbelt before he pulled out of the lot and onto the road. "Anything?" I asked. I could use a public kiss to shut London up. Would he be willing to do that?

He chuckled. "Do you have something in particular in mind?

I bit my lip. This thing between us was new, and the only people who knew about it were Cayla, Madi, and us. "Kiss me in front of London. That should shut her up about my man-eater guppy lips."

His smile dropped. Nothing but the faint sound of his music filled the air until he let out a long sigh of a breath. "I don't think we're ready for that."

"Why not?" I asked. My heart sank into my stomach. I wanted to prove to London and everyone else that I wasn't the pariah they made me out to be. I needed to prove that a boy could like me for myself too.

"Just...not yet. Okay? How about hanging out at my house? I'll even take a shower, brush my teeth, and put deodorant on." His grin returned and he added a wiggle to his eyebrows.

I let out a giggle. Maybe I was pushing him. He still wanted to hang out, so it wasn't a rejection. Right? He wasn't ready to go public...*yet*. A grin spread across my face, and I gave him a sideways glance.

He reached across the cab and laced his fingers with mine.

He had my full attention. I watched the smile on his lips grow, and he gave me that look I was beginning to recognize. The one that said he wanted to kiss me. "I need my babysitter to entertain me."

19

"I have some news," Cayla announced on our way to our foods class. "Logan's mom is having a barbecue tonight for the baseball team." She let out a little squeal.

I knit my eyebrows together as I tried to dodge the bodies in the hall and figure out why a baseball barbecue was a big deal. "So?" I shrugged.

"So..." She gave my arm a squeeze. "The softball team is invited too. Since we're both going to state!"

"Yeah?" Other than school and softball, I hadn't been to functions where I would be subject to peer interaction. But Roan and I were a thing now, and I could do it if he was by my side.

She rounded the corner and added, "No girlfriends or boyfriends. Team only."

"I bet the girlfriends aren't too happy about that," I said with a chuckle.

She let out an evil laugh.

We entered our foods class, giggling over her crazy laugh, making our way to our table.

"It's the first I heard about it. When did you find out?" I asked.

"First hour." She pulled her hair back at the nape of her neck and tied a hair band around it. "You guys are going, right?"

I pulled my hair back too, and said, "I don't know."

"You have to. I want to see James' face when you walk in holding hands." She threw her arms around me, jumping up and down. "Your first party as a couple."

Nerves danced around my insides. People started to stare. "Shh." I leaned closer. "Everyone is looking at us."

Not so shy anymore, Cayla shrugged it off. She used to be the shy one. I was the outgoing one. Now I stayed home from parties and she begged me to go. Had our personalities reversed?

As the bell rang, she said, "You can put all your doubts about Roan being embarrassed to rest after tonight."

"I don't know. He doesn't want to kiss me in public yet. He might not even go." I wanted that. Maybe he would hold my hand or something. That alone made me want to expose myself to a party where James, London, and Tommy Styles would be.

She rolled her eyes and groaned. "I know," she said. "Wear something nice the boys will drool over."

"Cayla," I said, tilting my head. "Guys don't drool over me. Besides, Roan hasn't even mentioned it."

She grinned and pulled out her phone, tapping on the screen. I caught a glimpse of Madi's name and the SOS message to get me ready for the party. "They will tonight. If Roan doesn't go, you're going anyway."

Mrs. Danes handed out the recipes, calling our attention to class. I wondered why Roan didn't tell me about it.

CAYLA CLOSED HER LOCKER AND SHOT ME A GLUM frown. "I guess I'll see you later," she huffed. She had an art project she had to finish before the end of the day. When she signed up for her senior classes, she put down art, thinking it was going to be easy. It didn't turn out that way for her.

"You'll have fun," I said in a peppy, "you got this" voice.

She rolled her eyes and moped off to her creative destination.

"What's her problem?" Roan asked, planting a hand on the wall above my head.

Boy, did he smell good. "She has another art project

due," I answered, closing my locker and then leaning my back against it. Roan looked extra nice today in his gray Lucky shorts and his Mighty Lions softball T-shirt. He said he wore it because he believed in me, in my pitching.

He chuckled. "Everybody knows art isn't a blow-off class."

I shrugged, looking up at his golden eyes. "I tried to tell her."

Our gazes locked and my insides turned jittery. Was he going to kiss me? Here in the hallway? In front of all these people? Yes, please.

"You look—" his eyes washed down my body and back— "great."

He said that when I got in his truck that morning. The way he was looking at me now, his voice, was causing my breathing to tick up a notch. *Thank you, Madi, for finding another outfit for me.* I swallowed and croaked out, "Thanks."

He grinned and kept staring at me with his golden kiss-me eyes.

A nervous giggle spilled over my lips. "You look pretty great too," I said. "Especially in that T-shirt."

"Tutoring you has been the best," he said, pausing. He dipped his head closer to me. He was about to say something else, maybe even plant a kiss on my lips, but was interrupted.

"'Sup, Martin? You on for Logan's tonight?" James asked, clamping a hand on Roan's shoulder.

My chin dropped to my chest so fast, it might have left a bruise. Did I want Roan to kiss me? *Oh, yeah*. But just the presence of James freaked me out. I had managed to stay away from him in the halls since prom. There he was, interrupting Roan and me.

Roan cleared his throat, dropping his hand from the wall to his side. "Uh, yeah. I'll be there," he said.

"You gonna be there, Tommie?" James asked.

I focused my eyes on Roan and James' loafers and the white and gray floor tiles underneath. I shook my head.

A puff of forced air came out of Roan before he said, "I'm in the middle of something. Catch up with you later."

James cleared his throat, pausing before he said in a strained voice, "Sure, man. Later." I watched his feet pass in front of me and disappear out of my circle of vision.

Kissing noises filled the air. The kind mean junior high boys created when they teased. The kind I had heard more times than I could count since prom. I glanced up in time to see a group of guys pass by, including Tommy Styles and London Hauser. This was probably the first time anyone had done that around Roan.

Roan reached through the clique and nabbed

Tommy by the back of his shirt and tugged him our direction. The rubber on the bottom of Tommy's expensive shoes squeaked across the floor. "You got a problem, Styles?" Roan asked with a growl.

I stood frozen in place, hiding my face but peaking up at what was going on.

Roan could be intimidating when he wanted to. Styles' wide eyes said he was nervous. "No, no problems here."

"Do that again and I'll make it too painful to even pucker up," Roan said through his gritted teeth. "Got it?"

Everyone in the group left Styles behind except London. She shot me a glare, but I ignored her. Styles went into panic mode, waved his hands, and stuttered, "Th-that wasn't me. I didn't—"

Roan dragged him closer and got in his face just as James stepped back into the picture. Roan's eyes narrowed even more.

James hovered next to Roan and growled, "Answer the man."

Why did James put his nose in this?

"Mr. Lowe, Martin, Styles, do we have a problem here?" Mr. Dade, our vice principal asked with his stern authoritative voice.

My breath caught, waiting for what was about to go down. The hall had cleared except for the five of us and a couple stragglers that passed by, gawking the whole time.

James took a step back and shook his head. "Nope."

Roan released Styles' shirt but kept his eyes glued on the jerk. He answered Mr. Dade. "No, sir."

Styles straightened his Lacoste V-neck shirt. "I, uh…" He paused, took a step back, glancing between Roan and James. He said, "It's all good, Mr. Dade. On my way to lunch."

Mr. Dade planted one hand on his hip and pointed down the hall with the other. "You best be on your way, then," he said.

A smirk spread across Styles' face as he gave the vice vrincipal a two-fingered salute. London looped her arm around Styles as they strode down the hall toward the cafeteria.

"And what are you three doing?" Mr. Dade asked. His eyebrows arched high on his forehead while he waited for an answer. He was a man of few words, or so I'd heard.

It was hard to miss that Mr. Dade worked out. He always wore the standard suit pants, shirt, and tie, but they didn't quite fit him right. It made him seem more intense. But I understood having a body that was hard to find clothes for.

"On our way to lunch." Roan's words pulled mc out of my assessment.

"Yup," James agreed, shoving his thumb in the opposite direction he was facing. "Lunch."

"You're too close to playoffs to be getting in trouble, gentlemen. You too, Miss Jenkins," Mr. Dade warned.

I nodded like a bobble head, but words wouldn't come out. Getting in trouble was never my thing. Not a good idea to start now.

The guys both answered in unison. "Yes, sir."

Roan hooked his arm over my shoulders and put us in motion toward the cafeteria. It wasn't a boyfriend kind of move because he'd been doing it all my life. At least since I've known him. Even that year when I was taller than him.

He whispered, "Freaking Styles. You okay?"

I nodded. If I ever had the thought my prom humiliation would end, Styles and London proved otherwise.

James fell in step beside Roan.

Why didn't James mind his own business? He made it worse. He never cared about anyone making fun of me before.

"I can take care of Styles myself," Roan grumbled.

"Yeah, I know," James said.

The tension surrounding us was so thick. If my muscles tightened any more, they'd have to place me in traction. I could feel Roan's muscles at attention around the back of my neck too.

The mood didn't change until we'd gotten our food, and James finally split off to sit with Logan. I could finally exhale all the way.

With my food in tow, I headed toward the outside doors when Roan said, "Let's sit with Gabe and Summer today."

I stopped. The thought of leaving the safety of my secluded table outside had my stomach twisting. Okay, it wasn't totally secluded, but there were only a few tables and they were a lot farther apart than the ones in the cafeteria. And after what just happened, I didn't want to hear the whispers.

"Come on," he said. "It'll be a practice run for tonight."

There was no way I was sitting by myself. I stared longingly at the table outside. If Cayla didn't have her art project, Roan could sit with whoever he wanted. But he was probably right about getting practice. I looked back to him.

Roan grinned and said, "No one's going to mess with you." He led the way, and I followed close behind, noticing Summer's friends, Bailey Garber and Harper Tisdale, were with her too.

Jett Bryant and Bentley Neilson, Bailey and Harper's boyfriends, took the seats we were going for. They were both on the hot guys list Cayla and Madi hounded me to make when the whole tutoring idea came about.

I nudged Roan's back and hissed, "There's not enough room."

Summer glanced up with a smile as Roan drug two

extra seats to the table. "Hey, Tommie," she said. "Great game last night."

It was a good game. Not only did we get hits every inning, I pitched good.

"Yeah," Harper said. "Congrats on the win."

I smiled and sat down. "Thanks. Couldn't have done it without my catcher." My gaze shot to Summer.

"Thanks, girl." She gave me a wink and said, "Catchers are like football linemen. We don't get the hype or glory, but without us, where would the team be?"

Roan reached over and bumped fists with her. "Absolutely," he said with his face beaming.

The other girls snickered.

Gabe pulled Summer to his body and kissed her cheek. She fit into him like a broken-in glove. "That's my girl."

It was so sweet, I almost sighed out loud. I looked at Roan, but he was too busy stuffing his face to be aware of me or their affection. I scanned the table and noticed how the guys paid attention to their girlfriends. A touch, a whisper—it was obvious they were together.

Roan wasn't like that with me in public where there were people we knew. My gaze roamed the cafeteria, watching the couples interact. When I came across James, two tables away, I caught him staring right at me. It wasn't a passing glance, and he didn't blink away. I did though.

I shot my gaze down to my food. Why was James staring at me?

———

WHEN I CAME HOME FROM PRACTICE, A NEW OUTFIT was laid across my bed. "Madi," I called, staring at the cream and black pinstriped shorts with a drawstring tie and a black V-neck blouse. It looked sophisticated but sporty at the same time.

"You like?" Madi asked.

I turned to see her with a big smile across her face, leaning against my door frame.

I was sure my grin matched hers. "Yeah," I said, holding the shorts against my waist to see if they would fit. "Did you get this?"

She crossed the room and draped her arm on my shoulder. "Isn't it great? I've been doing online research and found some great sites with prices we can afford. Mom's treat."

"Wow. You didn't have to do that, but thank you." I reached around her waist and gave her a side hug.

"I enjoy it. Like, a lot. I think I might do something with clothing for my career." She leaned over and smoothed the blouse out. "So I guess it's me and Brendan for supper tonight?"

"Yeah. Sorry I can't make dinner," I said.

She shrugged. "Big bro's ordering pizza. You need to get in the shower. Your beau turns into a bear when he has to wait too long."

I didn't know what had gotten into Madison the last couple of months, but I liked not having to be on guard with her. "Thanks for the outfit."

She shooed me into the bathroom. "Hurry so I can do your hair and makeup."

After I showered, Madi blow-dried my hair, parting it on the side and pulling it back.

"You have pretty hazel eyes. Let's bring out the green and show them off." She put a layer of nude color and then pink on my lids. And then she lined the top in a dark brown with matching mascara.

"Is this what you use?" I asked, looking in the mirror. It was still me, only better. It looked natural, as if I didn't have makeup on.

"Yep. Pretty girls don't need a ton of makeup. Just enough to highlight your goods." She tittered a laugh. "I sound like I know what I'm talking about."

"I think you do," I said, in awe of what she had done. "Because look at me."

She pressed her lips together and stared at my reflection. "Are you trying to make me cry?" she sniffed.

Crying wasn't my intention. If she cried, I would probably cry too and ruin her masterpiece. I let out an evil cackle and said in a wicked witch voice, "No, you hateful witch. Now let me out of here."

It worked because she giggled and said, "That's better. Don't forget lip gloss." She held the tube up. "Should you surprise Cayla or send her a pic?"

"Surprise," I answered, slipping the tube out of her fingers and applying it to my lips.

"Toms, you ready? We're going to be late," Roan called from the hallway.

We stepped out of the bathroom and he stopped dead in his tracks.

His eyes trailed down my outfit a time or two before he closed the distance between us, wearing a toothy grin. He didn't even say a word, just pressed his lips to mine. And after a few seconds I had forgotten Madi was even standing there.

Roan finally pulled away and whispered, "We should go."

"Have fun, kids," Madi said with a wave.

I wasn't sure, but I thought I caught a hint of red on Roan's cheeks. It was hard to tell with his tanned complexion. He laced his fingers with mine and we descended the stairs.

Brendan crossed the house from the kitchen, eating from a cup of yogurt. "Where are you going?" he asked and glanced at our hands.

Roan slipped his fingers from mine and shoved his hands in his pockets.

"We have a barbecue for baseball and softball tonight," I said. "Last-minute thing."

Brendan nodded once and took another bite. He eyed us both with a puzzled look on his face.

"See you later," I said. He didn't say another word. It wasn't like him not to make small talk with Roan, but maybe he could tell we were in a hurry.

Roan opened the door and stepped out. I followed, closing the door behind me.

"You didn't have to dress up," Roan mumbled as he opened the passenger door to his truck.

"Madi found a new outfit. She said it looked good on me. You don't like it?" I asked, climbing in and doubt following me. I closed the door as he headed to the driver's side.

I sent Cayla a quick message we were on our way and turned my gaze toward the row of houses on my side of the street. Maybe I should go change.

Roan got in and sighed. "I didn't mean it like that," he said. "It's fine."

I turned back to see his smile, but it wasn't his big relaxed, life-is-good smile. More like the forced, "I'm uncomfortable" kind.

I was about to ask what "fine" meant, but he leaned over and kissed me. "You look real pretty, Tommie Sue."

My muscles loosened. Did I get the signals wrong again?

He started the truck and eased from the curb.

On the drive to Logan's, he suggested we do some pitch and catch in the morning to get me ready for the first game of the playoffs. We talked strategy and focus and he held my hand the whole time.

We pulled onto Logan's street and it already had vehicles lining the curbs. Big two-story homes dotted the large lawns three or four blocks long. It amazed me how nice the homes were in this part of Sweet Water.

"Doesn't Wes Schultz live around here?" I asked, gawking at the manicured lawns and exteriors. Wes' family had so much money, they had their own airplane. I had never even been on one.

"Yeah, he lives beachside." Roan removed his hand from mine, pulled into a spot along the curb, and parked.

I opened my door and Roan met me before my foot hit the concrete. He shut the door as I smoothed the fabric of my outfit. The aroma of grilled meat hung in the humid air, causing my stomach to growl.

Roan chuckled and asked, "Hungry?"

"Sounds like it," I popped off with a grin. The food at lunch lost its appeal after I noticed Roan didn't act like the other guys at the table with their girlfriends. It was the same as it had always been. Friends only. At least in public.

He looped his arm around my shoulders and put us in motion. "Let's get some grub."

A few cars drove by as we walked toward Logan's house. A truck parked on the opposite side of the street ahead of us. A guy stepped out and jogged across the road. The way his hair glowed in the sunlight, it had to be Shawn Nelson.

He and Roan had a special pitcher-catcher bond. Hm...kind of like me and Roan? Was that what we had? No, it had to be different. That kind of bond didn't involve kissing.

By the time Shawn crossed the road, he was only a couple feet in front of us.

"Hey, Tommie. How's it going, Roan?" Shawn asked.

Roan separated from me and reached for Shawn. "Great, man." They did the bro hug thing. "You ready to put down some food?" Roan asked.

So the bond included hugging and patting his rump. Good thing I knew the ins and outs of baseball culture or I might have been jealous.

Shawn chuckled, rubbing his hands together. "I'm definitely putting a dent in the burgers tonight."

By the time it was all said and done, Roan had Shawn on one side and me on the other. We both had his arms resting on our shoulders. Not romantically inclined in any way.

As we neared Logan's house, chatter and laughter

filled the air. I pulled my phone out to send Cayla a quick message asking where she was.

There was a sign on the front door that said, "Come on in."

Shawn opened the door, pausing before he stepped in. "Ladies first," he said before motioning for me to go ahead.

"Thanks," I said and slipped from under Roan's arm to step into the house. I didn't want to break our connection, but I didn't want to be rude either.

My teammates, Dylan and Bailey, stood by the archway above the open kitchen. I scanned the house and understood what my mom was going for with her do-it-yourself remodeling. Everything was light-colored from the ceiling to the floor. Different textures and colors but still light.

Roan's hand grazed my back, and I turned to look at him by my side. Maybe tonight would be different. Tonight would be the night people would see I was girlfriend material.

20

This could be the last pitch of the game. A grin tugged at the corner of my mouth.

Summer gave me the sign that said, *Give me everything you got*.

I breathed in the heavy earth in the air, kept my form, and gave everything I had on the last pitch.

"Str-ike three!" Ump shouted.

Summer bounced to her feet, threw off her mask, and rushed toward me. The batter turned and moped toward her dugout.

Suddenly, I was bombarded with congrats on my shoulders and back from my teammates.

Summer jumped, wrapping her arms and legs around my body. "You did it! You did it!"

I wrapped my arms around her. "We did it!" I yelled back at her. My first no-hitter. The first game of playoffs was a W. My chest filled with so much pride and accomplishment. Tears began to stream down my face, and there was nothing I could do to stop them. All the pressure I'd carried for the last two days released.

Ice was back.

We bounced up and down. Me, Summer, Addison, Cayla, everyone, celebrating our win. Thanks to Cayla, I wasn't the only one who had a few tears flowing. Even Summer had two streaks down her cheeks where tears had washed the dirt from her face.

When the jumping had calmed, Summer said, "I've got to go hug my man." She took off for the dugout. Gabe and most of the guys were there, waiting along the fence.

"Girl, you were so amazing!" Cayla wrapped me up in a hug. "Summer's hand has got to be on fire from that last pitch."

Laughing, I said, "I don't know about that." I raised my hand for her to smack. "No-hitter, baby!"

She slapped my palm. "Your dad will be so proud."

My whole face felt like it was smiling. I couldn't wait to tell him. I turned toward the fence to find Roan. He and James were side by side with their arms stretched high and fingers hooked in the fence, looking my direction.

Coach called us all to the outfield for our team meeting before we got too crazy with celebration.

When we finished up, Cayla and I ran to the dugout

to get some money for a snack and drink from the concession stand before they closed.

"Toms," Roan said, walking toward the dugout with his arms wide open.

I snatched the money out of my bag and ran toward him, laughter bubbling inside me the whole way.

He scooped me up in a bear hug, twirling me around. "You were so awesome! A freaking no-hitter!"

His breath on my neck sent chills down my spine. I squeezed my eyes shut, memorizing the moment, and hoped he would kiss me right here in front of everyone.

When I opened them, the guys were headed our direction. Roan heard their ruckus, put me down, and took a step away. I knew that kiss I hoped for wouldn't happen.

James rushed in to hug me. "You were freaking hot," he said. I stood there with my arms pinned to my side. I gasped at his actions. Roan took another step backward, shoving his hands in his pockets. When our eyes met, he looked down at his feet. My breath stuck in my throat until James put me down.

When James released me, Gabe said, "Nice job, Jenkins." He patted me on the back. Summer was tucked under his arm. He didn't come to a lot of our games because he had to work at the business his family owned, Home Run Park, but it was always perfectly clear how much he was into Summer.

The baseball team, including Roan, surrounded me, offering congratulations like they do with one of their own...heavy-handed pats on the head and shoulders.

Even though it was a little rough, actually hurt, I couldn't keep the smile off my face. A no-hitter was a big deal for me.

Coach shooed the guys away. "Sorry to break up the party, boys, but it's time to get going. Ladies, pack your gear and get on the bus."

I said my thanks to the guys. It was the first time I didn't have that sinking feeling in my stomach, antici-pating a not-so-funny comment about my stupid public prom kiss. I trotted back into the dugout to get my bag. Cayla waited by our bags with a drink in each hand. She grinned and said, "You looked busy, so..."

I slipped the drink from her fingers and said, "Thanks, girl, I owe you." I slung my bag over my shoulder.

She winked. "I got you covered."

"Come on." I leaned an arm on her shoulders. "Let's get on the bus before Coach gripes us out."

We headed out of the dugout and made our way onto the bus. The next game was the following day, and Mazzie was up. The team counted on her and London to lead us to another victory. Since I pitched the whole game today, my pitching tomorrow would be limited.

The bus was full of chatter and laughter. Now that

the game was over, thoughts of Roan filtered back in my head. It brought a heaviness to my chest. The celebration inside me faded. It could have just been the emotions getting the better of me. I needed to let my family know how everything turned out.

Dad had sent one response to the messages I sent about the team going to state. I couldn't wait to see him at graduation. I sent him the first message.

> **Tommie**: Dad, you won't believe it! I pitched my first no-hitter. It felt so good. We won our first playoff game!

Who knew when he would answer? Maybe he was traveling home. I hoped.

I sent a group message to Mom, Madi, and Brendan.

> **Tommie**: We won!!! And I pitched a no-hitter!
> **Madi**: Gasp! We have to celebrate!
> **Madi**: Mom's at work.
> **Brendan**: Nice! Knew you could do it.
> **Tommie**: Yeah, Mom sent me a message she got called in.

Mom took every last-minute job she could get. Wednesdays were supposed to be the night she made a family dinner. I knew why she worked so much, but I missed Dad too. We all did.

> **Tommie**: I think we're grabbing food at the Burger Barn.

I sunk into the seat and closed my eyes.

"What's the deal?" Cayla asked. "You get your first no-hitter and all of a sudden you've gone from party girl to pouty girl."

I peeked one eye open and then closed it, adding a shrug. "I think the adrenaline high wore off," I said.

"Already?" she huffed. "You won't mind if I sit with the other girls while you zone out or whatever?" she asked.

I opened my eyes, flicking my fingers in the air, and said, "Go ahead."

Cayla plopped back into the seat beside me. "Tommie, you should be bouncing-off-the-walls excited."

I sighed. "I know. I'm excited. Was. It's just..." I sat up and turned toward her. "Did you see how the guys acted toward me after the game?"

"Yeah, they surrounded you like you were the star. Which—" she gripped my shoulders and gave me a shake — "you totally were."

I giggled at her actions but shook my head." No."

The look in Roan's eyes when James hugged me and the guys coming up to us burned my brain. "I mean, they acted like I was one of the guys. Those weren't little taps on the head, you know. I'm not a guy. They've always treated me like I was, am. And Roan does too. When no one's around, he treats me so different. Like a girlfriend."

Things at Logan's party didn't turn out like I'd hoped. Roan was off with his friends all night. I guessed that was the point of the party, but I had hoped it would be different.

I watched Gabe and Summer all night like a creeper. I couldn't look away. The attention Gabe gave her...it was clear that Roan didn't see me the way I wanted him to. The way Gabe saw Summer.

No guy did.

Roan may have said he wanted to ask me to prom as a date, but when it came down to his friends knowing about us. he pulled away from me. And to top the night off, he didn't even notice I only gave him yes or no answers on the way home.

When I climbed into bed that night, I told Juju I had playoffs to focus on. I would not cry over Roan hiding our new relationship. I needed to channel everything into pitching the best game ever. And that was exactly what I did.

Cayla gave me a sad smile. "Oh, Tommie. If he

thought that, why would he have said you guys could have something really great?"

I shook my head. She didn't get it. "Forget it. I think my emotions are all over the place right now."

21

S oda shot out of Madi's mouth and landed on the ground next to my feet. Cayla's description of the last three batters of the game was too much for my sister.

I jerked my legs under my chair. "Gross. You almost spit on me," I griped. I had to admit, Cayla could be hilarious.

"I could hear her knees knocking all the way in the outfield," Cayla argued as she started in on another round of infectious laughter. Madi was still reeling from earlier. We were having so much fun that I didn't even care that I was around all the softball team outside of practice. In public. For the second time this week.

"What's so funny?" Roan asked, joining our group, leaning against the tree next to me.

"Cayla's exaggerating," I said.

Cayla stood. "You know me, Roan. Story teller extra-ordinaire."

Madi burst out in laughter.

"Let's get a refill, Madi," Cayla said as she stood.

"Sure," Madi said, standing from the plastic chair across the table from me. She and Cayla giggled as they stopped and talked to Addison on their way to the order window.

Roan took the seat Madi vacated. "You want to come over before you have to be home?"

"I probably should go home since game two is tomorrow. You have a game too," I said, taking a long drink of my strawberry lemonade.

He laid his hand on top of mine, skimming his thumb ever so gently. "I'd still like you to."

My body relaxed. I turned my hand and laced our fingers together. "Why haven't your grandparents come home yet?"

He grimaced and leaned back against the back of the chair. "Gramps' brother had complications. He's still in the hospital, so they plan to stay until he gets out."

My eyebrows squished together. It had been over a week since they left. It had to be a bad situation for them to stay. "They won't be back to watch your games?" I asked.

He looked down to our hands and shook his head. "Doesn't look like it."

Since his mom died, his grandparents had been the only steady support he had. I knew how it felt to not have a parent show up. "I'm sorry."

Shawn Nelson ran up to the table, calling for Roan.

Roan dropped my hand as if it was on fire and leaned away, putting space between us. My heart dropped too.

James was on Shawn's heels. "You're going down, Nelson," he growled.

Roan sat there while James chased Shawn around the tree and table, tossing threats about jalapeños Shawn had ordered on James' burger. If Roan hadn't acted like I was a disease, I would have laughed.

Roan stood and put himself between them to protect his pitcher.

Every little signal Roan gave led up to this. It was obvious now. There was no way I read all of the pulling away wrong. Or every other time Roan kept his distance when we were at school or church or around his friends. Being a couple with me embarrassed him.

While he sorted out their scuffle, I slipped away to Cayla's Jeep, texting her on the way.

Tommie: Please take me home right now. I'm in your Jeep.

The pain in my chest was real. Real heartbreak. I

opened the door and climbed into the back seat. She and Madi got in a minute later.

"You okay?" Madi asked.

No, I wasn't okay. My heart had just been kicked around in my chest like a soccer ball. In fact, it was still in the game and I needed to get out of here. "Yeah. I just want to go home."

Cayla started the engine and pulled out onto the road. Roan sent me a message.

Roan: Where are you going?

Tommie: Home. See you tomorrow.

My shoulder was sore. My head pounded. Most of all, my heart was bruised and shredded.

This was the best freaking day of my softball career. I pitched a no-hitter. My first. In a state playoff game. Then why did it feel like I lost?

Roan and I both had playoff games the next day. I couldn't think about divorcing my best friend right now. A tear trickled over the brim of my lashes, and I swiped it away. Tough girls didn't cry, even if they lost their best friend.

22

I wasn't one of those superstitious athletes, except for my socks. But last night's disaster with Roan pulling away once again must have been an omen. Mazzie got hurt in the third inning of our second playoff game.

The opposing team scored three runs before London got the third out that inning. I tried to coach her up, but she wasn't interested in anything I had to say. I could still hear her words echo in my head, "I don't need a guppy telling me how to pitch."

The bus ride home was so quiet, the roar of the engine filled the air. I didn't even want to listen to music. The team's hopes to be state champions were gone.

Cayla leaned into me as the bus left the diamond. "It wasn't your fault. If Coach would have put you in right away, we'd be celebrating right now."

I gave her a shrug. We were still making hits, but the

other team kept scoring. Our defense from the circle hurt us. My pitching was solid. And if we weren't so behind when she took London out, we might have won.

"That throw in the fifth inning was awesome," I said. "You had a great game."

The corner of her mouth lifted into a half-smile. "Thanks. Too bad it wasn't enough."

"Gah! I wanted to make it to the finals so bad." I glanced over at Coach Hayes and Mac. They were both slumped in their seats. Addison and Summer sat two seats behind them. Summer had to be black and blue after catching London. The ball was all over the place, including in the dirt. I had to give it to Summer; that girl knew how to protect the plate. She wanted this so bad too.

Now what? Would any of us have the chance to play in college next year?

I had no idea what I wanted to do after my senior year. Up until my first kiss went horribly wrong, I never wanted high school to end. Staying in Sweet Water may not be the answer for me anymore. What if I did go away to college? Would I get homesick? Would Roan be too busy for me if I did go to Tennessee?

Roan had his first playoff game today. I sent him a message as soon as my game was over.

Halfway back to Sweet Water, he texted me.

Roan: Sorry about your game.

Roan: We won! Six to two.

Tommie: Congrats!

Roan: Did Mazzie have a bad game?

Tommie: She took a line drive to the head. Her parents took her to the hospital. Coach thought she had a concussion.

Roan: Ouch!

Tommie: Yeah.

Roan: So Coach put you in?

Tommie: After London flubbed the game. I held the other team, but we weren't able to make up the runs.

Roan: Sorry you guys are out.

Roan: The guys are grabbing burgers when we get back. Shawn wants to talk strategy with us.

I groaned. Why did it always come down to me being one of the guys? The clothes Madi had me wearing didn't work. And I had been trying. What was the use? I felt bad enough from losing, I didn't want my other failures in life to be smeared in my face tonight.

Tommie: No thanks.

Roan: I'll swing by and pick you up.

Tommie: Congrats to you guys, but I'm not up to celebrating.

Roan: You want to hit with us at the cages tomorrow? Give me some pointers?

I used to think being one of the guys was great. If all I wanted was to talk sports, eat burgers, belch and fart, it had its privileges. But I didn't want Roan or any of his team to see me as a boy anymore.

Tommie: I'm not one of the guys! Okay? I. AM. A. GIRL!!!!!!!
Roan: What??? I know that.

I felt a little guilty sending it with an exclamation point—or seven. But he didn't seem to get it. I couldn't do...whatever it was we were doing anymore.

Tommie: Forget it. Talk to you tomorrow.

23

C ayla swung by and picked Madi and me up for school this morning since Roan and his team were hitting at the batting cages.

"Girl!" Cayla called. I was a few steps in front of her and Madi as we walked across the parking lot. "Your butt is rockin' those shorts."

When I woke up this morning, my mood was less than perky. I almost went back to my old wardrobe. Almost. After I screamed at Roan in my message last night, I didn't want to give him a reason to treat me like one of the guys by dressing like one. So I wore a pair of white, fitted shorts and a white top with lavender and pink flowers. That was the closest to girly I could get without wearing a dress or skirt.

I stopped, turned to see her, and gave her a giant eye roll. She stepped next to me. I wished it were true...that I looked good. After my team's loss and the silence from Roan after I message-shouted I am a girl, I felt more like a sack of rotting clams.

Madi raised her hand for Cayla to smack it. "I know, right?"

London's cackle sprang from beside a car nearby. She adjusted the strap of her designer bag on her shoulder. "You can put lipstick on a pig, girls, but she's still just a pig." The little monster went out of her way to brush by me and strutted toward the school.

She blew the game yesterday but didn't skip a beat when it came to demeaning me?

"You're such a poser, Lon, baby," Madi called out.

My mouth dropped open. I glanced at Cayla, and hers was the same. That just rolled off my sister's tongue? She had that talent with me, but with a girl like London?

"Ugh, she is such a jerk," Madi grumbled. "Don't listen to her. She's just jealous."

London jealous of me? That was laughable, but Madi's assessment made me stand a little taller. "Madi, that was..."

"Awesome!" Cayla finished.

Madi shrugged it off, but we giggled all the way inside.

Roan wasn't around at the first bell. And I managed to avoid him all morning. By the time the lunch bell rang,

I had hopes he would want to talk and say he wanted to be my boyfriend.

"Let's go to the game tonight," Cayla said as she shut her locker door.

I glanced through the hall for Roan but didn't see him. Even though I was mad at Roan, I still wanted him to win, for the team to make it to the finals. I pursed my lips and started toward the cafeteria for lunch. "Yeah, okay."

"Hey," Roan said from behind me. His hand brushed my arm. "Could I talk to you?"

I gave Cayla a sideways glance. "What is it?" I asked.

He gripped my wrist and tugged for me to stop.

I turned to face him and gave him a cold stare.

"We'll catch up with you," he said to Cayla but stared right back at me.

Cayla stopped too and folded her arms.

I waved her off. "It's okay."

Roan tugged me in the opposite direction I was headed, through the double doors that led outside, and away from prying eyes and ears.

I thought about ripping him a new one, but that wasn't the kind of person I was. Plus, I was still unsure about everything and secretly hoping he would apologize and ask me to be his girlfriend. I folded my arms across my chest and looked across the lawn, waiting for the words I was desperate to hear.

"You're not wearing my baseball shirt?" His voice was a mix of gruffness and hurt. He'd worn mine the day of my big game. A tinge of guilt swirled in my stomach. I should have worn my Lions baseball shirt, but I wanted him and everyone else to notice I am, in fact, a girl.

"I didn't want anyone to mistake me as part of the baseball team." As hard as it was, I kept my voice even.

"What's that supposed to mean?" he asked sounding like a grizzly bear.

I took a step back and angled toward him. His eyebrows hung low over his deep-set amber eyes. "It means, I'm not a boy. I've been trying my best to not look like one, and I'm tired of being treated like I am."

He worked his jaw to the side and shook his head. "No one thinks you're a boy. I don't know why you keep on saying that."

"Is that so?" I tilted my head. "Then why do you treat me like I'm your buddy?"

He tilted his head too. "Because you are."

My arms dropped to my sides, and the sting of tears hit me faster than a line drive. "Exactly."

He raised his hands in the air and said, "I don't get what the big deal is."

I clenched my jaw. He was still my friend. I needed to ask him straight up, "Are you embarrassed for people to know about us? Is this all we are? Kissing buddies?" I thought I could be tough, strong, but the heaviness on my chest, tightness in my throat, and burning eyes showed me otherwise.

His mouth opened and closed. "No. It's not like..." His golden eyes searched my face before he looked over my head and rubbed the back of his neck. When he turned his gaze back on me, he was in full intimidation mode. "You're the one who wanted a kissing tutor," he said and let out at growl. "Look, I don't have time for this. I need to focus on tonight's game." He stormed back into the school.

COMING HOME STRAIGHT AFTER SCHOOL WAS bittersweet. It was nice to come home and not rush the rest of the night to get everything done. At the same time, I knew that would wear off by next week and I'd be missing softball. My career was officially over.

Mom sent a group text to Brendan, Madi, and me over my lunch period to be home no later than six that evening. Dad was supposed to call from overseas, and Mom wanted to have "supper" together.

I lay on my bed, staring at the ceiling, when my phone buzzed. I checked the screen and saw a message from Cayla.

Cayla: He looks good.

She sent a few photos of Roan catching and batting. Guilt squeezed my chest. Roan was right. I was the one who wanted a kissing tutor, but I didn't expect to have that kind of chemistry with him. He had sent me a message while he was on his way to the game to ask me to come. It was an hour drive, and even though I wanted to support my friend, I couldn't miss Dad's call. Besides, I knew Mom wouldn't let me skip out on it even if I wanted to. He wasn't too mad at me if he sent that message, but that made me feel even worse. Plus, his grandparents were still gone. I was the only family he had.

I went down to the kitchen a few minutes later to help with supper. Juju crossed the kitchen from her water bowl to the stairs and curled up in front of them. She waited there for me sometimes. I stirred the onions and peppers in the skillet. The patio door opened. Brendan came in with the grilled steak for fajitas. Madi had already gotten out all the condiments while Mom set the table. She had made progress on the wall she was opening up between the kitchen and living room.

Mom had propped up the tablet on the table while we finished cooking. It sounded with Dad's video call. Mom ran from the island to the table and pressed the button. I shut the burner off and skidded over beside her. Madi and Brendan did the same.

Dad's face appeared. He'd been sporting a beard for

a while. His eyes lit up at the same time his lips spread into a smile. "Hey."

Mom touched her lips. That meant she was getting teary-eyed.

"Hi, Dad!" Brendan spoke up. He seemed as excited as me to see Dad.

"Hey, there, Bren. You're looking good. Taller."

I peeked over at my brother. His face beamed like a little boy.

"Hi, Daddy," I said, taking my turn.

"Tommie girl." His eyebrows raised. "I believe congratulations are in order for your no-hitter. I'm impressed."

My chest swelled with pride. I knew it would. Making my dad happy always made me want to do it more. "Thanks," I said with the biggest grin that would fit on my face. I glanced down. "But we lost the next game." It still hurt, losing. Knowing my softball career was over didn't help. "I thought we were going to win this year."

"A no-hitter, kiddo, is fantastic. I'm sorry about not winning the playoffs, but sometimes we don't get what we work so hard for." Dad's eyes darted around.

I stepped away so Madi could take my place.

"Madison? Goodness, you're growing up."

"Yeah," she said softly. Her voice a little off.

Dad asked, "How are your grades?"

"A's. Just like you wanted," she said.

He nodded. "Good girl. Angela, babe, I'm sorry I don't have time for a meal, so let me talk to each of you. Okay?"

"Oh, sweetheart," Mom said. Her voice cracked at the end.

Dad gave her a tight smile. "I know. Something came up."

She nodded. "Who first?" she asked.

"Tommie? You want to go first?" he asked.

I nodded.

Mom handed me the tablet and I headed for the stairs. I had something private I wanted to talk to him about. We started with the usual chit-chat. As I climbed the stairs, Juju joined me. After I told him all about my no-hitter, the conversation turned to college.

"How am I supposed to know what I want to do for the rest of my life? The past six years have been all about softball. Now that's over. I feel kind of lost already." I grabbed a pillow off my bed and hugged it.

"You'll find it. Open yourself up to new things. Try something different when you get to college."

I wanted a real answer, not a "you'll figure it out" one. "I guess," I mumbled.

"Are you wearing makeup?"

I bit my lip and nodded. I didn't know what he

would think about it. Eighteen is old enough to wear makeup and even my fifteen-year-old sister wore it.

"Are you trying to get a boy's attention?" he asked. "Or do you have it already?"

I glanced down at my comforter. "I don't know. Boys are...hard to figure out."

"Oh, honey," he said with a chuckle. "They're not that complicated. Trust me."

Dad always had great advice about everything. Even though I had never talked to him about boys before, I knew I could trust him. "Here's the deal. I like this boy. He said he likes me. We've kissed a time or two, but when we're at school or around his friends, he acts like we're just friends. You know? He's different when it's just the two of us."

"Ah." He scratched the back of his head. "What does your momma say?"

"I haven't talked to her about it yet. Please don't tell her, okay?" I asked.

He worked his jaw to the side and combed down the coarse hair of his beard. "I'll keep it to myself for now. But she's pretty smart."

I nodded. "I know, but I figured you're a guy, so you might know what I should do." I shrugged, even though it was a big deal to me. "I always read guys wrong. I think they like me, but they don't. I even started dressing better so they wouldn't think of me as a guy."

"I don't want you changing who you are for a boy," he said, using his authoritative dad tone. "For anyone. You hear me?"

I nodded. "Yes, sir."

"I guess it wouldn't hurt to swap out the athletic shorts. At least cut back to when you actually practice and workout." He raised his brow to make his point.

"Madi basically said the same thing." I sighed. I knew I was frustrated with how things had been going and didn't want to be grumpy with Dad. It wasn't his fault or Madi's. "She helped me find some clothes that fit me."

He smiled and the corners of his eyes crinkled. "Good. I'm glad you two are getting along."

"Me too. But what should I do? About this boy."

"Men are simple creatures. We aren't intuitive like women. If we were, I'd better understand all the women in my life." He let out a chuckle. "That's for sure."

I giggled too, shaking my head.

"Boys need a direct approach. We often need things spelled out for us. Especially a teenager who's still green when it comes to girls." He let out a soft chuckle. "I may not be an expert on women, but I've learned to pick up on things. It took me years to get that far. If you're not sure about something, you just need to come right out and ask."

I thought I was direct with Roan. Last night in my

message and then today at lunch, but maybe I wasn't. "Thanks, Dad."

"But make sure he's being a gentleman," he said and gave me a hard-edged Marine look. "You understand? And you be a lady."

I nodded. "Yes, sir."

"Let me talk with your brother."

"Okay," I said, sliding off my bed, and headed downstairs. "You're going to make it for graduation, right?"

"I hope so," he said.

My shoulders sagged. That wasn't a yes. "So that means no." Dad not showing would be the rotten cherry on top of this senior year.

"It means I'm trying, but I can't promise." His eyes teared up, and I felt worse for saying anything. "I love you, Tommie girl."

I sighed, wishing I could have one of his hugs. "I love you too."

Cayla had the cruise control set on our way to Raleigh, North Carolina. Since I let Madi sit shotgun, she was in charge of the music.

Madi checked the GPS on her phone. "Oh, good. Only thirty minutes until we're there. I have to pee again."

"You went like thirty minutes ago," Cayla complained.

"It was over an hour ago," Madi said. She picked up her coffee and took a sip. "This latte makes me have to pee. I can't help it."

My phone buzzed. I had placed it face-down on my thigh after I'd checked a thousand times to see if Roan had responded to my good luck message earlier. We didn't talk after his game last night. And after talking to Dad, I concluded the timing was bad. It wasn't fair for me to dump on him the day of his game. They had a serious chance of being the next state champions. I probably should have waited until state was over to say anything.

I picked it up and saw Roan's name on the screen. My heart beat faster. At least he sent me something.

I opened the message and read it.

Roan: Thanks, Toms. You're coming, right?

My whole body sighed. He's still talking to me.

Tommie: Yep. Should be there in 30.
Roan: That makes me happy. You're my good luck charm. Gotta go before Coach catches me with my phone.

A zing shot through my heart, knowing I was still his good luck charm. The same zing I felt when he told me I was his good luck charm while we sat in his hot tub. I hoped after this game I would be more than a student of his.

How much longer could I ride this rollercoaster of emotions?

THE CROWD HAD BEEN ON ITS FEET OFF AND ON since the first inning. Roan hit a two-run home run in the sixth inning. He gave me our sign that he heard me on his way toward first base. After he ran the bases, he pointed at me. I pointed back. Cayla and Madi were jumping up and down next to me, screaming. It was so exciting. In my heart, I was holding on to his public expression for me.

James hit a homer in the seventh. Our eyes locked after he landed on home plate. I think. Not sure how he even saw me in this big crowd, but the smile on his face was beautiful. I loved seeing the team winning and having so much fun doing it.

Gabe hit a two-run homer in the seventh. Summer went crazy, doing a two-fingered kiss over and over. Gabe did it back, and every softball team member that was in our row swooned. It made my heart sigh.

Roan had been so quick and agile behind the plate. I was so proud of him. It was finally the bottom of the ninth inning. Every able-bodied person in the Lions stands was on their feet. Cayla, Madi, Summer, Harper, Addison, and me were stomping our feet, clapping our hands.

We were up eight to six. Anything was possible, and the guys had to be on alert for anything. It was even the top of their lineup. The best guys were ready to bat. Coach Crawford had gone to the mound to talk with

Shawn. The Blue Racers had just scored three runs in a row on him. Coach kept Shawn in.

Their best hitter stepped into the batter's box. He dug his feet into the dirt and readied his bat. He popped one right over the third baseman's head and made it all the way to second base.

Shawn took his hat off, wiped the sweat from his brow, and fit the cap back on his head. The sun had beat down all morning. It was so hot, moisture clung to my skin just sitting in the stands. The runner on first stepped off, taking one step and then another, slowly inching further from the bag.

"Throw him out, Roan," Madi yelled.

"It's risky," I said. "If the throw is off and goes past the second baseman, the runner has a chance to make it to third. That would make it easier to score."

"Oh, yeah," she said and then pressed her fingers to her mouth.

I totally believed in Roan. He was in the zone. "Roan's been hot today though," I said. "If he feels it, he'll do it."

Madi and Cayla nodded in agreement. They had their hands , watching the field.

I cupped my hands on either side of my mouth and shouted, "Woo, Martin."

Shawn gripped the bill of his cap, adjusting it, checked the sign and gave a nod. He checked the runner.

CHAPTER 24 | 197

Wound up and delivered a ball just as the runner took off.

Roan popped upright on his feet in a flash and threw the ball to second base. The runner dove for the base as Carter Patterson caught the ball and tagged his hands.

The infield umpire watched the tag unfold. He made a fist and called, "Out!"

Lions fans roared. Game over. The Lions were state champions.

Roan did his hip action move he made after each win and ran toward the mound. Shawn mimicked him.

The Lions dugout emptied on the field to the mound and bounced up and down, shouting, patting their hands and gloves on top of each other's heads.

My heart swelled with pride. Roan had worked so hard to make it that far. I laughed as happy tears filled my eyes, watching him. His future at Tennessee was solid. I wished his grandparents could have been here.

Cayla, Madi, Summer, and the girls high-fived and had our own celebration on our way toward the dugout. We waited for the team to return. Neither the embarrassment from prom nor the hurt and frustration I had with Roan mattered at the moment. The spotlight was on the Lions baseball team—the new North Carolina state champions.

Parents and girlfriends inched forward to hug their players. Cayla, me, and the girls stood back and waited our turn. Roan scanned the crowd. His dark hair was a sweaty mess, sticking up from the mask he had to wear. A sheen of moisture covered his deeply tanned skin along with streaks and smears of dirt where he'd wiped his hands. I secretly loved the way he looked after a game. It was rugged and masculine.

His smile, frozen on his face from winning, faltered until he saw me. Butterflies flittered in my chest. He weaved in and out of the players and their families to the only family he had present...me.

My smile had to have matched his. He scooped me up, burying his face in my neck.

"You were so awesome. You're a champion," I said, holding him as tight as he held me. His chest shuddered against mine. Working so hard toward a goal and then achieving it brought on all kinds of emotions. I felt it after my no-hitter.

He held me for a little while before he whispered, "Toms."

I kissed his ear, which was the closest thing to my lips. He slowly placed me back on my feet.

Madi gave him a giant hug too. "Such a great game. Congrats!"

"Thanks, squirt," he said, his smile still as wide as it could be.

Cayla did the side hug thing as she said, "Nice game, Roan. You guys deserve it." She let go of him and latched on to Madi, pointing toward the fence, and saying, "We're going this way."

I nodded and looked up at Roan's unwavering winner smile. I could get so lost in those lips if he would let me.

He pulled me into another hug. "I'm so glad you're here," he said, tickling the skin of my neck with his breath.

I held him close and rubbed his back, storing the moment in my heart. "I wouldn't miss it. I'm sorry your grandparents weren't able to be here."

He pulled away, shaking his head. "It's okay. They probably won't make it to any games next year. I need to get used to it." Disappointment flooded his tone. His eyes focused on something behind me and he took a step backward, rubbing his palms down his thighs.

"Roan," James called as he stode beside us. "Party at my house tonight." He placed his hand on my arm, giving it a squeeze and then let go.

I pulled my arms closer to my body, shrinking away.

He spoke to Roan but kept his eyes on me. "Bring Tommie with you. You'll come, won't you?"

I looked at Roan, silently asking what I should say. He shifted his weight from one foot to the other, but said nothing. I wanted to be there for Roan if he wanted me to but going to James' house wasn't ideal. I was still getting used to being around the baseball team again, around James, without the stupid prom kiss video playing in my head or on the tongues of others.

Even though we went to Logan's party together, it wasn't like he acted like we were anything more than what we'd always been growing up. One of the guys.

He shook his head as if he were coming out of a daze. "Okay. Uh..." He turned to James. "What time?"

James' grin grew. He rubbed his hands together. "Seven. And Nelson wants your sister to come too." He took a step back and said, "Save me a dance, Tommie."

My mouth dropped open. Shawn Nelson is the guy that's been asking Cayla to go to the games? Wait, save James a dance? Did he want to dance with me or was he reminding me of what happened at prom? I embarrassed us both that night. Since then, I hadn't even been able to sum up the courage to face him. We had two short encounters, and that was two too many.

James spun around and met up with the coaches.

Roan groaned.

I focused back on Roan as he scrubbed a hand down his dust-powdered face, leaving finger swipe marks behind.

Did Roan not want me to go? "I don't have to go if you don't want me to. I'm surprised he'd want me anywhere near him after what happened at prom."

Roan searched my face, his expression pained and full of confusion. He opened his mouth to say something right when Coach Crawford whistled and shouted for the boys to grab their gear and get on the bus.

He inched closer. Nervous jitters bubbled in my stomach at his movement. I couldn't figure out if he wanted to kiss me or tell me something. Madi and Cayla returned.

"I'm thirsty," Cayla said, interrupting whatever Roan was about to do or say. "Let's get a milkshake before we get back on the road."

She and Madi chattered, but I stayed glued to Roan, waiting for him to say whatever was on his mind.

"Martin," Coach Rojas called. "Let's go."

His shoulders dipped. A push of air rushed out of his nose. "I...I've got to go," he said, pointing his thumb behind him toward his bag still in the dugout.

I nodded. "Okay. I'm not driving, so we can message. If you want."

"If it's not too crazy on the bus." His eyes moved toward the girls as he stepped backward. "Thanks for coming." He gave us a small wave and then walked away.

25

Madi prattled nonstop the entire drive to the party from the back seat of Roan's Toyota truck. He said she was invited too. For once, I didn't mind that I wasn't alone with him. I wasn't sure Roan even wanted me to go.

Madi picked out the cute wrap dress I wore and fixed my hair. I shouldn't have been so negative about her going. It wasn't like she and Roan were strangers. He'd been hanging around our house for years. We were all practically family.

Ugh. That made me like a sister too. Not what I was going for.

Madi finally quieted as Roan knocked on the door. I knew she was excited, but I had to shoot her a look over my shoulder to make it happen.

The door opened, and I quickly turned back around

to face the tall man who answered. His hair was the same reddish-brown as James'. He was old enough to be his dad but didn't seem as old as mine.

Mr. Lowe stood straight and tall in his stylish clothes. I didn't know much about fashion, but they looked expensive. His lips parted, lifting and stretching wide when he focused on Roan. "Roan," he greeted, jabbing his hand toward him. "Great game today."

Roan met his hand, gripping it for a firm handshake. "Thank you, sir."

Mr. Lowe's eyes glided to me, then to my sister, and then back to me. He quirked an eyebrow. "Miss Jenkins?" he asked.

Heat flamed my cheeks as I dropped my gaze to his white button-down shirt and gray shorts. He probably didn't recognize me without my mouth open, swallowing his son's lips.

I gave a nod and answered softly, "Yes, sir."

"You look a lot like Tommie. Are you her sister?" he asked. I assumed he was talking to Madi because there was no way I could make eye contact again.

Roan spoke up. "This is Madi. Tommie's younger sister. She's a freshman."

"It's nice to have you lovely ladies. Please come on in." Mr. Lowe stepped back to allow us in the house.

I wanted Roan to go first, but he ushered Madi and me in. My stomach clenched as soon as I stepped inside.

What was I doing? This was such a mistake. Did I think I could just dive into the shark-infested waters of James Lowe and teenaged gossip?

Madi nudged me further into the house, whispering, "Keep going so he can shut the door."

I heard Mr. Lowe ask Roan in a low voice, "Both your dates?"

Roan chuckled, but Shawn Nelson came speeding toward us, and I didn't hear what else they said.

"My man," Shawn said, rushing Roan for a bro hug. Shawn was hyper tonight. I imagined they all were after such a big win.

Roan didn't get ruffled too much, but he was talkative with Madi on the way over.

"Ladies," Shawn said, checking me and then Madi out. He whistled and started to say something, but Mr. Lowe cut him off.

"Mr. Nelson," Mr. Lowe said in a reprimanding tone. "That is not how you behave toward a lady."

I stifled a scoff, wondering if he thought himself exempt.

Shawn cleared his throat. "Yes, sir." He bowed his head, placing a hand over his heart. "Forgive me. Your beauty stunned me."

Madi giggled.

"That's better," Mr. Lowe said with a chuckle. "Roan, Shawn, show our guests outside, will you?"

Oh, my gosh. James acted more like his dad. Although, James wasn't nearly as formal, he could be arrogant too. But wow, he was more handsome than his dad. Better built too. His dad may have been a lady's man in his day though.

Roan led us through the house to the living room French doors. It was similar to Logan's house with the colors and beachy style, but more formal.

Summer and Gabe were standing at a wall of windows. They were so close as they could have been mistaken for conjoined twins. The way Gabe focused on her, held her close, was what I craved from Roan. She didn't even notice when I waved.

After the door was closed and all four of us were outside, Shawn turned to us. "Sorry if I embarrassed you or anything. Mr. Lowe is..."

"Different," Roan finished. He touched my upper arm, letting his hand slide down before he shoved it in his pocket. "Want some food?" he asked.

I wasn't hungry but nodded and answered, "Sure."

"Madi?" Shawn asked.

Her smile brightened. "Yes, please. Whatever is fine."

Roan and Shawn headed toward the outdoor kitchen.

I scanned the backyard as the salty ocean breeze blew the strands of my hair. With my hair down, it made me feel ten degrees warmer. "It's so hot," I mumbled to Madi. "I should have put my hair in a ponytail."

"Nuh-uh," she barked under her breath. "No ponytail. You look good with your hair down."

I pursed my lips. It wasn't the heat that made me cranky. I sighed and said, "Not sure I belong here."

She hooked my arm in hers and started across the lawn. "Don't be silly. Can you believe this place? It's gorgeous. And this backyard is huge compared to ours. Could you imagine having the beach right behind our house?" She sighed and opened the gate for us to walk through from the yard to the sand. "We could run every day right here."

I snickered, imagining it. "Yeah, it would be nice."

"Look," she said. "Tonight is going to be a good night. Relax for once. Remember how much fun you used to have doing stuff like this? You'd come home, and I begged you to tell me everything."

I gave her a pointed look. "Yeah, then you'd start a fight."

She shrugged. "I was jealous."

"It's not as fun as it used to be," I said as I put us in motion toward the water. Evan, Carter, and another baseball player passed us going back toward the house. They all had shorts and a Lion's baseball shirt on. I looked down at my dress. "Are we overdressed or what?"

"Uh, no," she said quickly. "Roan dressed nice. Did

you see what Mr. Lowe was wearing?"

I shrugged. "A white shirt."

"Not just a white shirt. An Armani white shirt. And the cut of his shorts...I'm sure they were Dolce and Gabbana."

My eyebrows rose on my forehead as I looked at her. "You know Armani and Dolce and Gabbana when you see it?"

"Don't make fun. I like fashion." Her grin spread across her face as she dipped her head.

She was good at picking clothes out for me, that was for sure. "So, Shawn Nelson?"

"Yeah," she giggled. "It's new. He's sweet. And funny." She let out a little sigh.

"Did you just sigh?" I teased, squeezing her arm to my side.

"Shut up," she groaned, leaning into me with a smile that said she'd been caught. "Did you see how heads turned when we walked through the house and yard?"

"No, but that always happens when you're around," I said. "They probably feel sorry for you that you have a jock for a sister." My words came out short and snippy. It wasn't a revelation Madison was prettier than me. I'd always known that. It was easier to deal with when she wasn't trying to compete with me though. But I was the one failing at the moment.

She steeled her eyes. A growl rumbled in her throat

before she said, "You're so stupid sometimes." She turned and fled toward the house.

My stomach sunk. Great. I circled my arms around my middle. Was this how the night was going to be? I squeezed my eyes shut and listened to the waves rushing the shore. *Jealous much, Tommie?*

She was right. I was on track to ruin the night. Roan asked me to come, and I needed to stop being afraid. If he didn't understand what I meant about not wanting to be one of the guys, I would show him. Even if there was a risk of a prom kiss repeat.

The sun warmed my back as I listened to the waves rolling in. The scents of charcoal and grilled meat wafted through the air. It was late for supper, but I supposed people who lived in the big houses on the beach worked long hours to afford such places.

My skin prickled as if someone was watching me. A hint of a familiar sweet cologne swirled around my nose. I opened my eyes to turn around and bumped into a hard body. "Oh!" I jumped. It startled me to see James at my side.

I took a step back. My eyes darted away from him to the sand, and I apologized, "Oh, I'm sorry. I didn't know you were there."

He chuckled. His gritty voice rang out, "It's okay." He handed me a clear plastic cup full of ice and a dark liquid. "I thought you might like some sweet tea."

I glanced at his blue eyes. The heat on my face amplified. I took the glass. "Thank you." He brought me a drink? Did Roan send James with it? My head was full of questions and no answers.

I took a sip, sneaking an inconspicuous look at James. He wore a custom Sweet Water Lions baseball jersey. Much nicer than the school's baseball uniform. His shorts seemed fancy like his dad's.

"My parents insisted on having this party. I preferred a bonfire down at the beach. No parents." He grumbled the last part and took a drink of his own cup.

My heart had inched itself up to the base of my throat. One by one, my muscles tensed from my head to my toes. Even though I toyed with the idea of asking him to try kissing me again, I never would have had the guts to do it. I didn't want to face James again.

All I could think about was prom and that stupid kiss and running away from him on the dance floor. How I never apologized for doing that. I blurted out, "I'm sorry."

He looked down at me, eyebrows scrunched together. "It's not your fault they wouldn't let me do the bonfire."

I shook my head and swallowed down my nerves. "I mean," I turned my gaze to the ice in my glass, "about prom. That was so humiliating."

"Yeah." He chuckled. "Speaking of that, here." He

handed me the official prom photo we had taken at the dance.

My stomach automatically sunk, thinking about that night. I'd forgotten all about the photo booth setup with the photographer. Any fun we had was overshadowed by my fish-lips plastered all over the screen. My face heated as the image burned my brain.

"Why did you leave without saying anything?" he asked. "I've been wanting to talk to you about it, but you're never alone."

"Tommie?" Roan's voice called out from behind us.

James mumbled, "See. Never alone."

Thank god Roan showed up. I turned away from James and gave Roan a look that said he got there in the nick of time.

"Roan," James said. The inflection came across as if he didn't want him to be there.

Roan carried a cup and a plate of food. His warm amber eyes questioned me. When he was close enough, he handed over the plate, and stood on the other side of me.

"I already brought her a drink," James said.

"Yeah?" Roan asked, looking between us. He took a stuffed mushroom off the plate I was holding and popped it in his mouth.

I shuffled my feet so close to Roan, my arm pressed against his. We stood there without talking. My stomach tightened, and then my chest tightened, and the thought of eating any of the fancy food on the plate made me nauseous. What the heck was going on?

"James. Roan," Mr. Lowe called out.

I kept my eyes focused on the ocean, willing James to leave and Roan to stay.

"Dad probably has some speech he wants to give," James said with a huff. "We should go."

I felt him brush my elbow, and I stiffened.

Roan chugged the contents of his cup. They both stood still as if each was waiting for the other to make a move.

The sunlight filtered in rays that streamed across the water. I leaned a little closer to Roan and breathed in deeply, hoping to catch a whiff of his sweet, musky scent. Just a hint. My fingers brushed his in hopes he would lace ours together, but he didn't move.

Mr. Lowe called again. James groaned and turned, waiting for us to join him in the short trek back.

"Let's go," Roan said softly. And we turned to follow James.

James opened the gate to their backyard and motioned for me to go ahead.

I made an excuse to check on Madi to escape the weirdness that was going on. What was James' deal? Was he setting me up for something?

26

I stood next to Madi along the wall of windows that faced the beach in James Lowe's house. The sky across the ocean was a deep blue as the sun began to set. All the baseball players gathered around the backyard listening to toasts from Mr. Lowe and the coaches.

I glanced at my sister. We both held plates with weird food on it. Slimy stuffed mushrooms, toasted bread with green relish-looking stuff on top, and tiny quiches. The quiche didn't look so bad. She took a bite of one. A soft giggle bubbled out of her as she covered her mouth and chewed. Her long golden hair was perfect as usual. The soft smile on her lips twitched before she glanced down and refocused on someone in the crowd.

I scanned the guys to see who she might be looking at. Roan, James, Shawn, the pitcher, and Davis the shortstop took turns looking our direction. Ugh, London was there with Tommy Styles, the jerks who loved to make fun of me. They wouldn't dare do anything at James' party with Roan here. Not after Roan's threat in the hallway at school.

My stomach hadn't stopped aching since my snippy comments to my sister on the beach. She was probably trying to be nice, but it was just a lie. The guys didn't turn their heads to watch me when we walked through. They didn't do things like that for me. They did it for Madi.

I got jealous of her and didn't even realize it.

"Hey," I said, waiting for her to look at me.

Her eyes flitted to mine. Looking at her was not like looking in a mirror. Her eyebrows arched, but no words escaped.

"I'm sorry about earlier. I didn't mean to be such a...rip."

One corner of her mouth lifted before she shrugged. "You were a rip. It's frustrating that you think like that about yourself."

"You're my sister. You're biased." I waved it off. "Anyway, I'm sorry."

She nodded toward a seating area near the grass. "Let's go sit."

The sun was setting, casting dark shadows onto the backyard from the house. Lanterns and lighting scattered throughout the seating area and walkways flickered on as we weaved through people.

Mr. Lowe announced a special highlights video in the media room. The coaches and most of the players filtered inside, including Roan. An old Lions baseball game played on the television in the outdoor living room near the house. A TV mounted outside by my patio would be nice. I tucked that in the back of my mind to drop a few hints to Mom about getting one. Probably wouldn't happen soon since the living room was a wreck.

When we made it to the sitting area, the game playing on the TV was replaced by a blue screen. I ignored it and sat down in an empty chair next to Madi. This fancy food was gross. I only carried my plate around because I didn't have anywhere to put the photo. I sat the plate on the table, making sure the picture was underneath.

"This place is beautiful," Madi said. "This must be like an outdoor kitchen and dining."

The grill was built into the bar along with a griddle and refrigerator. "Yeah, it's really nice." I knew James' family had money, but I didn't realize how much. I scanned the backyard, taking everything in.

Some of the players came back outside. I caught sight of Shawn heading our way. A tinge of jealousy clenched my chest. He was the star pitcher, but he came over to sit with Madi. They weren't even dating yet. Madi didn't have problems talking to guys.

Not long ago, talking to boys wasn't a problem for me. If we talked baseball, or any kind of sport, I could go all night long. But if I was attracted to them, I clammed up. At least my senior year, anyway. And especially after being humiliated at prom. Now I felt like a pariah.

My phone buzzed. I pulled it from the small pocket of my dress and ducked my head to see who was calling. Dad. My chest tightened.

I looked up at Madi and interrupted her conversation. "Dad's calling."

Her eyebrows rose.

We both stood at the same time and I answered, "Hello?"

"Hey, Tommie girl," he said. "How's it going?"

Madi stepped closer so we were inches apart. Worry haunted her expression.

"Is everything okay? Are you okay?" I asked. Dad rarely called out of the blue. He had been injured before, and that played at the forefront of my mind.

"I'm fine," he said. "Don't worry about me."

I closed my eyes and let out my breath. The tightness in my chest released. "He's fine," I whispered to Madi.

"Hi, Daddy," Madi said.

"Hi, kiddo."

"Hold on, Dad. We're going somewhere quiet so we

can hear you." I nodded to the darkened corner of the yard that looked to be empty and quiet enough for us both to hear him.

Madi looped her arm around mine as we hurried our pace.

"Where are you? It better not be a party," he warned with a playful tone.

"It's parent-approved," I promised as we reached the quiet area. I tapped the speaker button. "Can you hear us okay? Is there too much noise?"

"Ah, I can hear the ocean. I miss that," he said.

"What's going on, Dad?" Madi asked. A light from the back of the house cast a soft glow on her smooth cheek. Worry held her expression.

"I have a new unit coming in next week. I'm sorry, Tommie. It doesn't look like I'll make it home for your graduation."

My eyelids fell closed, and everything from my heart to my stomach seemed to follow suit. Tears instantly stung my eyes.

Madi's hand touched my forearm. She asked, "What about the week after that?"

"Not with a new unit," he said. His voice wavered a bit. "Maybe at the end of summer. I really miss you, but there's nothing I can do to change the situation."

I swallowed and tried not to breathe, hoping that

would keep the tears in place. "It's okay," I muttered. "I know it's not your fault."

The Marines was all Dad had ever done since he graduated from high school. He loved it. Sometimes it felt like he loved it more than me. It took all of his time. Time he could have spent at home on the weekends or evenings. Even if he weren't deployed, he would be gone a couple weekends a month.

"Tommie girl, I wanted to be there. I'll make it up to you." His voice was soft and pleading and how could I get off the phone without him knowing I was about to cry?

Madi pulled me into a hug.

After I said nothing, he added, "Okay?"

Whooping and laughter erupted from the outdoor television area where we had been sitting.

I cleared my throat to speak, but Madi's gasp stopped me.

She pulled her arms away. I opened my eyes and saw her hand covering her mouth. "Don't look," she whispered.

"Tommie? Madison? Are you still there?" Dad asked.

I followed Madi's line of sight. People gathered around the TV by the seating areas. A few people pointed at the television, snickering. Some glanced back at us. Two bodies blocked the screen.

"Yeah, I'm here," I said as I stepped back to view

what was so funny. "It's o—" I caught a glimpse of the TV screen and my words disappeared. The official prom photo of James and me was side by side with the one of me swallowing James' lips like a guppy fish.

My gut twisted. The gelato curdled in my stomach, which threatened to empty its contents on the lawn. I swallowed it down. "It's okay, Dad. I've got to go. Bye."

I hung up just as London slithered out from the small crowd of people. She shot me a smirk before her mouth formed an O and she did a Betty Boop pose with her finger poking her cheek and her butt sticking out. I had to get out of there.

Summer came into view, heading my direction while Gabe split toward the TV. "Tommie," Summer said.

Madi's arm came around my shoulder. "She's such a b—"

"Stop." I raised my hand. I needed to get out of here. "Where's Roan?"

Gabe barreled through the crowd and shut the TV off. He grumbled something and dispersed those standing around.

Summer answered, pointing a thumb behind her. "He was in the media room. We just left there. It's down the hall, second door on the right."

I wiped at the tears that leaked over my lashes. The door to the house seemed a mile away. I rubbed my stomach, not sure I could make the walk of shame without losing it. "Could you keep London away from me?"

Summer rubbed her palms together. "I'd be happy to."

"I'll help," Madi growled. She squeezed my shoulder. "You okay by yourself?"

I nodded.

"Let's go," Summer said and spun around.

Madi joined her. London saw them coming and skirted closer to Styles, who was talking with a group of guys.

One foot in front of the other, Tommie.

I repeated the mantra until I reached the inside of the house. Women's voices drifted from the kitchen. My face was sure to be red and splotchy, and I didn't want them to see me.

I thought this night would be one where Roan and I would go public as a couple. Not be a reminder of prom.

Dad should have been home for my graduation, but he was still in Afghanistan.

My stomach twisted, and I pressed my hand against it. Almost there. I crossed the room quickly and quietly to the hallway.

"Come on." James' voice echoed down the empty hall.

The voices lowered. I followed the low rumble. Was it the second door on the left or right? The first door was a bathroom. I peeked around the second door on the right. Professional baseball, basketball, and football jerseys, all framed, hung on the three walls I could see. A screen hung from the ceiling with a baseball game playing from a projector, also hanging from the ceiling toward the back of the room.

Roan and James stood between two rows of black leather theater-style recliners. Both had their arms folded tight against their chests.

"Just own up to it," James said.

Roan shook his head. "That's not what happened."

James' bicep flexed before he said, "I was sitting in my car, waiting for the rain to die down. I saw you."

"We're friends. That's it." Roan stood as still as Adonis.

"Looked like more than that to me." When Roan didn't respond, James let out a curse and then chuckled. "So what are you saying? It's a friends with benefits thing? How long's this been going on? Because she sure didn't act like she'd been kissed at prom."

Roan's arms unfolded. His hands moved to clamp his waist as he squared up to James.

I stepped back around the corner and flattened my back against the wall of the hallway. Tears fell as my chest twisted even more. Were they talking about that day we went to the batting cages at Home Run Park?

Roan kissed me in the rain. It was so amazing, I

didn't remember saying one word on the way home. That definitely wasn't a kissing lesson. And neither was the hot tub afterward.

"It's not like that," Roan said.

My eyes burned with the tears I'd been trying to hold back. I needed my best friend. But there he was, denying that he kissed me. Denying that we were anything but friends.

My chest shuddered. I couldn't hear another word. I escaped back down the hall to the entry and bolted out the front door as a sob slipped out.

I didn't think anyone saw me. The warm night air clung to my hair. It was probably limp and stringy after the walk on the beach. I swallowed and swallowed, holding off the shame as I fled down the sidewalk to the road.

Roan drove. I could call Cayla, but I didn't want to explain what happened. Not until I was away from the party. I rushed down the road. My sandals clopped against the pavement. At least there was no traffic, no one to run into.

As I passed the fancy homes, tears, increased until my vision blurred. That didn't stop me from leaving. This was the worst night of my life.

Dad chose another Marine unit over coming home for my graduation. To Dad, I was just a mouth to feed.

London and the others continued to rub my nose in the stupid prom picture.

My baby sister got more dates her freshman year than I had my whole life. Even got invited to the party and by this point I was sure my invitation had been a mistake.

And my best friend was ashamed to admit he kissed me.

Everything Roan told me was a lie. I would always be Tommie the Tomboy. Nothing but one of the guys. A buddy. The girl who fish-lipped James Lowe at prom.

Even though my feet burned with the start of blisters, I ran all the way home. When I reached the front steps, sweat covered my skin and dripped down the middle of my chest. I clasped my fingers together on top of my head and tried to catch my breath before I went inside. The scent of sweat mixed with gardenias filled my nose. It was cooler at James' house with the breeze blowing in from the ocean, but I wanted to be as far away from there as I could get.

After a few seconds, I reached into my pocket for my phone to send Madi a message, but it wasn't there. Did I leave it? Drop it?

Ugh. I couldn't believe it. Prom was nothing compared to the events of tonight.

My eyes stung with another round of tears ready to spill. I had to get inside before a neighbor asked me what was wrong. I found the hidden key, unlocked the door, and climbed the stairs to the bathroom. As soon as I shut the door, I flipped the lock and tried to breathe.

I knew I had to look like a wreck since I cried most of the way. I probably ruined the dress from wiping my snot on it. I went straight to the sink to rinse my face with cold water. It didn't help that I was a shaking, out-of-breath mess with a broken heart.

I turned on the faucet, cupping my unsteady hands underneath, and splashed my face a few times before shutting it off. It helped to slow my breathing some. I reached for the towel and patted my face dry.

That had to have been close to a three-mile jog. In sandals. Ugh, my feet burned. Skimpy shoes were not made to run in.

I eased my butt onto the counter and slipped the strap off the back of my heel, wincing. The trashed shoe dropped to the floor. My breath caught from the pain. I did the same with the other and inspected the source of the pain. A large blister was forming on the ball of my foot, another on my big toe, and one on my heel where the back-strap had rubbed. I checked the other foot and found the same.

I thought cool water might help. I turned on the faucet again, soaking my feet in the sink. A tear fell from the corner of my eye, and then another. It seemed I had an endless supply of them. I wiped my cheek and shut the water off. A knock sounded at the door.

"Tommie?" It was Mom. "Is that you?"

I sniffed and cleared my throat, hoping she couldn't tell what a mess I was by my voice. "Yeah."

"Are you okay, sweetie?" she asked. "Madison says you're not answering your phone."

Was I okay? My chest shuddered, bringing on a flood of tears and snot. *I'm not okay. I'm a total reject.* "I lost it."

"At the party?" she asked.

"No, I don't know. I'm sorry." My voice cracked at the last word.

"Are you sure you're okay?" she asked, concern weaving through her voice.

I sniffed and swallowed. "Yeah. I'm going to take a shower." I needed one. The back of my neck was matted with my sweaty hair. I hadn't even looked in the mirror. I was afraid to.

I eased my feet onto the cool tiled floor. Ouch. I sucked in a breath through my teeth. That would not work. I rolled my feet against the floor until the weight rested on the outer edge of my soles.

The door handle rattled as if Mom was about to come in, but I had it locked. "Okay, then. Good night."

"Night," I squeaked, my voice not holding up from the new wave of tears. I took a step, turned on the shower, and stripped. There was no way I could stand in the shower. I'd have to sit on the edge of the tub.

After my shower, I crept to my room and closed the door to put on pajamas in the dark. The pain from the blisters on my feet was too much. I literally crawled into my bed. I wished Juju was in here to keep me company. I thought prom was the worst night of my life. Tonight topped it by at least ten times.

I curled up underneath my sheet with the box of tissues, wiping my already snotty nose.

At least James wasn't afraid to be with me in public. Our kiss might have been humiliating, but not as bad as falling for your best friend and then finding out he lied about feeling the same way.

Sob after sob took over. My body shook with every one. Loneliness settled in and made my insides ache in places I didn't even know existed.

A gentle hand rubbed my arm.

I turned to see my mom taking a seat on my bed. I hadn't even heard her come in.

"Oh, Tommie," she said softly. Her fingers moved the damp hair from my face. "What's wrong, sweetie?" Her gentle voice and touch released even more hurt, and I couldn't stop crying.

Maybe the thing from tonight was all my fault. I was the one who opened my mouth like a fish when James tried to kiss me. Who could resist making fun of something like that? Dad expected more than what I produced. I should have tried harder to have as good of grades as he wanted, like my sister. And I was the one who pressured Roan to help me find a stupid kissing tutor and then agreed to him teaching me. He was the one who wanted more. He led me on. Best friends shouldn't lie to each other.

"I-I'm a-a f-fail-ure," I squeaked out between gulps of air.

Her hand stroked my cheek. "You're not a failure." She continued to soothe me by combing my hair back with her fingers. "Tell me what happened."

When I could speak without a constant shudder of my chest or break in my voice, I spilled everything. The humiliating prom kiss. The kissing tutor. About Roan saying how good we would be together. I told her Dad would rather stay and train a new unit than come to my graduation. And the rotten cherry on top...how Roan was too ashamed to admit we were anything more than friends.

"Sweetie," she said with her gentle Mom voice. Her arms wrapped around me. "You should have come to me when all this started. You can always talk to me...about anything."

In that moment, when she held me close, rocking back and forth, my chest—my heart—hurt a little less. There was one person who loved me no matter what I wore, or how I looked. It didn't matter that I was a tomboy or didn't get straight A's.

My chest hiccupped, and the trickle of tears turned into streams again.

"Your daddy loves you. If it was at all possible for him to come home, he would drop everything to do that."

I knew he loved me. I knew he would come home if he could, but that didn't keep my heart from aching. "I-I know. It-just...hurts."

A few more sobs rolled through me.

"I know you're hurting but I promise things will be better in the light of morning," she said.

What did that mean? How was I ever going to feel better? I sat up and blew my nose. "How could Roan do this to me? I wanted to tell him about Dad not coming home and that stupid picture plastered on the TV, and he would make everything better like he always does, but..." I swallowed and squeaked out, "He might as well have punched me in the face."

"Tommie." Mom wrapped her arms around me again. My face pressed against her shoulder. "Don't say that."

"It wouldn't have hurt as much," I said against her shirt.

A soft knock sounded at my door.

"Please," I pleaded, gripping her shirt. "Don't let anyone come in. I don't want to see anyone."

The door opened. It didn't matter if it was Madi or Brendan. I didn't want anyone to know. I had to deal with this myself first. Brendan would tell me how dumb I was being. Madi never got rejected and wouldn't understand.

"Toms?" Roan called.

I gasped, shaking my head against my mom's shoulder. He was the last person on the face of the earth I wanted to see. I sat up, and my eyes narrowed in on the guy who had taught me to kiss. They guy who I'd fallen for. My ex-best friend. "Go away!" I shouted.

The light from the hall bent around his tall frame. His eyes widened, and his mouth opened. "Madi told me about London," he said, taking a step inside.

My vision got fuzzy with another onslaught of tears. Just when I thought I was getting a handle on it for the night, he showed up. "Leave me alone," I cried out, trying to be forceful, but it was more like a wounded animal.

"Toms..." He took another step.

"You don't get to call me that anymore. You've been lying this whole time. You're the one that said we could be so good but are too ashamed to tell anyone we're together."

His head snapped back as if I had slapped him. Guilt was written all over his wide eyes. His jaw dropped. Did he think I didn't know what he was doing?

I scoffed. "I heard you telling James we were just

friends. If that's what you want, fine." I sniffed and wiped the tears from my cheeks, calming my breath. "You were right about one thing. Letting you be my kissing tutor was the dumbest idea I'd ever had."

The shock on his face changed into something else that I didn't recognize. His gaze went to my mom, who stood up. His shoulders slumped at the same time his lips curved into a deep frown. I thought he would say something, deny it, justify it, lie, anything. He just stood there, staring in my direction, but no eye contact.

I turned away, lay back down, and pulled the covers over my head. It might have been a thirteen-year-old move, but I didn't care.

Footsteps padded away from me. "Tommie needs her privacy right now," Mom said firmly.

"I—" he said in a strained voice.

"You need to go home, Roan" she said.

I heard him sigh, and the door closed.

Madi was probably out in the hallway, watching the drama.

The sheet tugged down. Mom hovered over me. "I love you," she said, kissing my forehead. "Get some sleep. We can talk more tomorrow." She padded across my carpet and opened the door. "Juju's here. You want her to come in?"

"Yes," I croaked. At least Mom and Juju cared about me.

Juju whined beside my bed and I leaned over to pick her up.

"Goodnight, sweetie," Mom said and opened the door once more to leave, closing it behind her.

My eyelids slid shut as I fumbled for another tissue to blow my nose. The box was about half-empty by now.

I flopped back down and lay Juju in front of me on top of the blanket.

Faint voices came from the hallway. It was probably Madi asking what was going on. They were too soft to make out what was being said or who it was. It didn't matter because they soon disappeared.

With Juju by my side, I should have been glad they left me alone. It was what I wanted. But lying in the dark with the night's events playing on my heart...it was tough.

My life was changing too fast. I wasn't sure living at home after graduation would be a good thing anymore. Cayla would be busy with college and working more at her dad's store. The photo from prom wasn't disappearing. I lost my best friend. Maybe Aunt Jenny would let me stay with her for a while until I figured out what to do with my life.

The commotion downstairs signaled my family was home from church. No one had tried to talk to me since Mom came in my room this morning.

I threw my covers back and gingerly made my way to the bathroom. My feet hurt. My head hurt. My eyes hurt from crying so much. Juju had scurried out when Mom came in to check on me before she left for church. Mom said I looked like I had gotten into a fistfight, minus the cuts and bruises.

All the perfect little couples at church would have been a reminder that I wasn't girlfriend material.

Yeah, the blisters would pop and heal, but my heart?

I flushed, washed my hands, splashed some water on my puffy eyes and face, and patted it dry with a hand towel. There was no point in cleaning up more than that to lie in bed all day.

I rubbed my palms against my eyes and opened the door. Madi leaned against the wall across from me.

"Hey," she said with droopy eyes. I didn't know why she would be tired. She wasn't the one who cried all night.

"Hey," I croaked back. My throat felt like I'd slept in a sandstorm. I continued to hobble past her to my bedroom. I didn't even bother shutting my door because I knew she would come inside anyway. I crawled under my covers and waited for her barrage of questions.

Her footsteps came closer until the bed dipped by my feet where she sat and stared at me. "What happened last night?" she asked.

I shook my head. "I don't want to talk about it."

"Did someone hurt you?" Her big blue eyes were round and worried. She had on her tight shorts, tank, and sports bra she wore for jogging or working out.

"Did you wear that to church?" I asked, hoping to deflect a little.

It didn't work. "You look terrible." Her frown deepened. "Fine. I already know about stupid London and Dad. Mom said you had a fight with Roan too." She waited for me to say something.

After a minute of silence, I decided to be vague. It was embarrassing enough. I didn't want to be the laughingstock of the freshman class. "Something like that."

Madi let out a loud sigh. "What did he do?"

"I'm not ready to talk about it. Okay?" I didn't want to think about it either, but it consumed my thoughts.

She grimaced but nodded. "Okay," she said, standing. "Mom's making you chocolate chip pancakes."

"I'm not hungry," I said. It wasn't true. The hunger pains gave me something else to focus on beside the full heartbreak that was going on inside me.

The corners of her mouth tugged down. She gave me a long look and walked out of my room, closing the door behind her.

Part of me wished I had my phone to see if Roan sent me any messages. But I lost it somewhere between my house and James'. Probably for the best. I was sure I would have scrolled through pictures of him.

I wasn't even able to call Cayla. She didn't know about anything that happened since she didn't go to the party. She would want to cheer me up, though. And I didn't want to be cheered up yet.

I closed my eyes and tried to drift back to sleep.

My door burst open and banged against the doorstop. It startled me from my heartbreak coma or sleep, not sure which state I was in. I turned to see who was there.

"Girl," Cayla said. She folded her arms against her

chest, popping a hip out. "Am I not your best friend? Why didn't you call me last night? You shouldn't have walked that far by yourself."

She plowed across the room and opened my blinds to let the sunlight in. It shown directly in the windows and made me squint. My room faced west, so it I knew it was afternoon. Had I lain in bed that long?

Bikini strings tied around the back of her neck caught my eye as she stormed toward me and plopped on the side of my bed. Cayla twisted, bringing a folded leg up so she was facing me.

I sat up and scooted toward the headboard. I drew my knees up and sucked my bottom lip between my teeth and bit down. Was she mad that I hadn't called her yet?

"How did you find out?" I asked, moving my gaze to the pattern of the quilt on my legs.

"Madi," she said.

I pushed out a sigh, showing I wasn't happy about my sister blabbing. It should have been me telling Cayla. Hard to do without a phone.

"Spill. Tell me everything," she demanded.

She was the only best friend I had left, and she deserved to know. I didn't want to hold out on her, but I was secretly hoping Roan would come over and tell me the whole thing was a misunderstanding.

If it had been, he would've come over already. But he

didn't. Tears stung my eyes the millionth time since yesterday. I glanced at her soft brown eyes beckoning me to begin. So I did. About my missed kiss with Roan, our walk on the beach, his deflection at Gabe's question, my dad not coming home for graduation, London's hurtful prank, and Roan and James' conversation I overheard.

"Girl," she said and then wrapped me in a hug. "I'm sorry about your dad."

"It's okay. I know he can't help it." I swallowed. It was already easier to say. "I'll get over it."

"Ugh," she growled, releasing me. "London is such a rip. I think everyone is tired of her stupid face."

I pinched the fabric of my quilt along the seam. I had always tried to be nice to everyone, but she was so spiteful. "I don't know what I ever did to her."

"Nothing." She sighed. "She's a spoiled brat." She paused for a few seconds. "Stupid Roan," she growled. "I can't believe him." She looked up at me with an expression looking as painful as I felt. "I know he was your best friend too. I feel like I pushed you on him. But the way he looked at you, touched you, sometimes...I..." She dropped her head. "I'm sorry."

My eyes stung again. I shook my head. It wasn't her fault. "I thought so too." I wanted it—him. I had begun to feel something more with him since last summer, but I was too scared to do or say anything about it.

"I knew he was about as friendly as a grizzly bear

and only cared about what he wanted." She raised her head and looked at me. I met her gaze. Her lips stretched into a tight line before she said, "I just can't believe he would do that to *you*."

My eyes brimmed. Even though my throat tightened, I managed to speak. "Me either. He hasn't even tried to talk to me since last night." My words came out so soft, they were barely audible.

Her eyes glazed over when she asked, "Madi said you cried all night."

I nodded.

"You like him that much?" she asked.

Her question unleashed the floodgates. Tears flowed over my lashes like the rushing waves onto the beach. I bit my lips together and nodded again. "I don't want to be his secret. Kiss when no one's around and pretend nothing's going on when we're around others."

He should have never been the kissing tutor. I wiped my face. "I don't even care about boosting my reputation from prom anymore. He was more than a kissing tutor. More than my best friend. Now he's just a boy down the street. And he won't even be that for long."

Cayla, Roan and I had P.E. last period, but the school had an assembly celebrating the baseball win. Most all the softball players had Athletics P.E. at the time as the baseball players last hour. The entire school would soon be in the gymnasium for an assembly to celebrate the baseball team's win. My team sat together on the bleachers per Coach Hayes' instructions. We were smack in the middle of the bottom row.

After the rest of the school had shuffled in, the principal announced, "North Carolina's state baseball champions, Sweet Water's very own Lions!" The crowd cheered. Coach Crawford and Coach Rojas led the players across the hardwood to the lion's head in the middle of the floor.

Cayla leaned close and said, "Coach Rojas is hot."

I scrunched my nose, checking him out. "Ew. He's like... old."

"He's in his twenties. That's not old. Those tattoos. And he's... fit." She wriggled her eyebrows.

I snickered and shook my head. She was probably trying to put a smile on my face. It worked. For a second.

Roan and I had ignored each other all day. Even though I told him I didn't want to see him again, I was disappointed he hadn't tried to talk to me at all since Saturday night. He had to know how much he hurt me. I couldn't be the one to make a move. And obviously ten years of friendship meant nothing to him.

Coach Rojas made sure all the players were lined up between Coach Crawford and himself. Roan was the last one. His face was a blank slate. Shawn, James, and Gabe were whooping it up. Roan stood there like a statue with his hands in his pockets, his eyes focused on the floor in front of him.

"These young men," Coach Crawford began, giving a speech about their dedication and work ethic. He acknowledged Gabe's batting average for the playoffs, Shawn's low ERA, and Roan's ability to keep the ball in front of him and the pitchers focused.

A quiver of excitement vibrated in my chest at his accomplishment. Even though what he did hurt, I couldn't have been prouder for him. He was a great catcher. He worked hard to get to the level he was at.

Coach Rojas put a hand on Roan's shoulder. Roan's head swiveled to look at him. The corners of Roan's mouth lifted.

The tiny spark in his golden eyes had me drifting back to our first kiss. The quiver I felt seconds ago turned into boxing gloves that used my heart as a punching bag.

Roan faced forward and our eyes connected. His smile fell along with his gaze. He was back to his stone-like expression.

We were close to being so good. We almost made it as a couple. Close, almost...they never count.

30

"I should have studied tonight," I said. "It's my last two exams."

Mom slashed her hand above the steering wheel as she pulled into the parking spot. "Wednesdays are the only time I have free. Besides, I'm working doubles the next two days so I can be off this weekend." She reached over and squeezed my cheeks. "You're graduating from high school."

My sister chimed in too. "Come on. It'll be fun."

I didn't want to have fun. I wanted to study and mope about my miserable luck with boys. Not to mention the fact that I lost my best friend. Interaction with Roan today had been a repeat of Monday and Tuesday. Minus the assembly and brief eye contact during. Which meant we ignored each other.

"The new Tommie Jenkins will kiss high school and all its drama goodbye," Madi said, opening her door.

"I don't even know who I am anymore," I mumbled.

Mom placed her hand on my forearm, giving it a gentle squeeze. "Who do you want to be?"

I heard Madi shuffle back into her seat. The last few days, she'd tried to be extra nice. She even picked out my clothes for school and laid them on my bed when I was in the shower every day.

I shrugged.

"Girls." Mom glanced at me and then the rearview mirror. "You choose who you want to be. And then you be it. You want to be a straight-A student...you learn how to study effectively. You want to be a good athlete...you practice, practice, practice. You can be what you want, but it will cost you hard work. Dedication." She opened her door, stepped out with her purse in tow, and closed the door behind her.

Madi and I did the same, meeting her in front of the car. She wrapped an arm around both of us as we crossed the parking lot toward the clothing stores. "It's okay if you don't know what or who you want to be yet. Just remember God first and then family. Always. Everything else works around that."

Sometimes Mom dished out advice I didn't understand, but this was simple. It wasn't the first time she had said it, and I did my best to follow that creed.

We entered the first store. Graduating seniors had to buy a gown to go over our clothes, so I didn't think what I wore underneath was important. I went to the rack of dresses and flipped through them. It would probably be hot, so I looked for something lightweight and sleeveless.

Madi and Mom spread out where the tops and shorts were. After a few minutes of searching the rack, I went to find them. I thought we were looking for a graduation outfit for me. I think they had something else in mind.

"I have a room started for you," Madi said, ushering me toward the dressing room. She pointed to an open stall with a pile of clothes hanging on the hook. How did she do that so fast? "Try those on. I want to see each one on you."

I sighed. "I'm just getting a graduation outfit. I don't need to try on all that stuff."

Mom came up behind us. "Tommie, you need some clothes. Now go try those on."

I rolled my eyes but stepped into the room and closed the door. I stripped off my shirt and shorts and put on the first set I came to. A fitted T-shirt with a shimmery silver-gray bead design with swirls of black and pink, and a pair of black button fly shorts.

When I looked into the mirror, the odd familiarity of the moment hit me. I met Roan on the pier on a day just like this. The memory of walking on the beach hand in hand and the first kiss we shared played back.

I closed my eyes, and then I could feel the warmth of my hand in his. Our first tutoring lesson on the beach. The way my stomach quivered when he pulled me close...those feelings never stopped. I wanted more every time we were close like that.

My eyes stung. It was over. Wet streaks flowed down my cheeks. I wasn't sure I could trust another guy like that. Roan's rejection humiliated me more than my public prom kiss debacle. He broke my heart. Judging by the brief moment our eyes met at Monday's school assembly, he had an idea. At the rate he was responding, he would be gone to Tennessee and we'd never speak again.

I tried to shake his tender kisses from my mind.

"Let us see," Madi said, knocking on the door.

I opened my eyes and looked in the mirror. Tears stained my cheeks. My red eyes gave my misery away. Would I ever stop aching for him?

I sniffed and swallowed down the lump in my throat before twisting the knob and pushing the door open.

As it swung open, Mom and Madi stood, waiting to assess me. Mom's mouth pressed into a tight line. Her brow crinkled above her soft blue eyes. "Tommie," she said. Her tone was full of compassion. She stepped forward and pulled me into a hug.

"I can't do this." My words came out broken. Exactly

how I felt. "Why do I want someone who doesn't want me?"

Madi played music from her phone through the car speakers on the way home. My favorite song came on, and my throat instantly tightened. I closed my eyes and fought the tears.

Roan said he wanted me to think of him every time I heard it. And then kissed me during the whole thing. In his hot tub. I even ended up on his lap by the time it was over. Ugh, it was so amazing. I had felt so special in that moment.

I wiped the tears from my cheeks. I couldn't tell Madi to shut it off. Maybe I tortured myself by remembering every tremble in my stomach, every excited heartbeat, every electric touch. Why did we have to end this way?

After we got home, Mom pulled into the garage. I grabbed the bag of clothes off the floor and got out. I needed to study, but mostly I just wanted to lie down.

I followed Madi in the house and darted straight up the stairs. Brendan walked out of the bathroom when I made it to the hallway. He had on a pair of dark jeans, a nice shirt, and his wet hair styled in his messy way.

"Hey. Didn't expect you home this early," he said.

He looked down at his shirt sleeve as if he didn't want to look me in the face.

I shifted the bag in my hand. "Yeah. I didn't feel like shopping." I went on in my bedroom and dropped the bag by the closet. I plopped down on the end of my bed to take my shoes off.

Brendan leaned against my door frame and asked, "Do I need to have a talk with him?"

I stopped what I was doing. Did he know about Roan? About what happened? "Who?" I asked.

His face tightened. "Roan. I can't believe you two haven't made up yet."

I shook my head. This wasn't some silly, petty fight like we'd had before. This was him breaking my heart. I sniffed. Stupid tears wouldn't stop showing up. They flooded my eyes, distorting everything into a blur. "No."

"Let me know if you change your mind. I'm going out. Night, sis."

I slipped off my shoes and crossed my room to shut the door.

A knock sounded as soon as I closed it. I swung it back open. Madi stood there.

"Yeah?" I asked.

She guided me over to my bed for us to sit down together.

"What?" I didn't want to talk.

"I know you think Roan lied about liking you, but I

saw it. That night when he came over for supper. He flirted with you the whole time. It wasn't the first time either. I've seen him do it before. Before all this kissing tutor stuff. What about when he brought you home from prom and stayed with you? And then that night you guys went to the party at Logan's?" She pointed out to the hall. "He kissed you right out there. In front of me. And it wasn't some little peck on the cheek either."

Her reminder only cracked my chest again. "Please stop reminding me of him. It's over. I need to get over it. I need to move on, or I'll never want to leave the house again."

She gave me a sad smile. "I'm sorry. I just didn't want you to think—" She stopped before finishing her sentence. "Okay." She stood, walked to the closet to snatch up the bag of clothes, and said, "I'll take these downstairs and wash them."

She walked out of my room without another word and closed the door behind her.

I reached for my book bag by the nightstand and pulled out my pre-calculus notes. Not that studying would be possible. I couldn't stop thinking about him. How much longer could I take this?

31

For the fourth morning in a row my sister, had an outfit laid out on my bed after I'd showered. A small smile lifted my cheeks. She had been so different the past few months. It was her idea for me to find a kissing tutor. If I had kept my feelings in check, would it have worked out with Roan? Maybe I was pushing him before he was ready. It didn't matter anymore.

Even though I wanted to wear my old basketball shorts and a T-shirt this week, Madison made sure I didn't. And that was a good thing.

I slipped on my clothes and knocked on her door.

"Yeah?" she called.

I turned the knob and poked my head inside her room. "What do you think?" I asked, pushing the door all the way open and holding my arms out to my sides so that she could see my outfit.

Madi stood at her closet and gave me a smile. Her thick, golden-blonde hair was brushed and tussled with a few curls at the ends. She wore a pair of shorts that showed off her lean legs and a tank top with a short-sleeved shirt over it that had crisscrossed straps at the top. She motioned with her finger for me to turn around. I did so.

She gave me a thumbs up. "Fits well. Looks good. You'll knock 'em dead today."

I rolled my eyes. "It's just school."

Her eyebrows lifted. "You want me to do your hair? I'll just blow-dry and smooth it out." She met me at the door, turning me around, and combed her fingers through my damp hair.

"If it won't take too long." I considered going to Roan's house this morning, but he needed to apologize to me, not me to him. But I missed him. I missed kissing him. I missed having fun with him.

Madi nudged me in the shoulders. "Let's get with it. Don't want to be late for school."

After she blew-dried my hair every which way, she had me sit on the toilet so she could run a smoothing iron through it.

I sat quiet and still. Pretty much like I'd been since Sunday.

"Have you talked to him?" she asked.

I shook my head.

She combed a piece of hair out and smoothed the iron over it. "Have you seen him? He looks miserable."

I pursed my lips. "He's avoiding me. Which is fine. I didn't want to see him either. Besides, I'm the one who's miserable, not him. He got what he wanted." Even as I said the words, I couldn't believe they were true. Roan may have come off as distant or a growly bear to others, but they didn't know him like I did. If he was the same guy I'd grown up with, he wouldn't purposefully hurt me.

Would he?

My chest tightened. I didn't know anymore. Maybe I needed to hear why he didn't want anyone to know.

"Would you be mad if I talked to him?" She used the iron on the shorter pieces of hair near my jaw, curving the bottoms inward.

"Don't talk about me." I sucked in a deep breath but stopped when another wave of pressure squeezed my heart. I pressed my palm to my chest and rubbed.

Madi stepped back, staring down at me with her eyebrows knit together. "Are you going to cry?" she asked.

I let out my breath and dropped my head, propping my elbows on my knees, and rested my forehead in my hands. "Thinking about talking to him makes my heart hurt. Thinking about not talking to him makes my heart hurt. He's like family, you know. I don't think I can just walk away and forget him."

"Then don't," she said with a firm voice.

My brow furrowed, and I looked up at her.

She had that determined, focused look she gets when she's about to take the court in a volleyball match.

"What do you mean, don't?" I asked, standing.

She stepped back, unplugged the iron, and then pulled out a makeup bag from the cabinet under the sink. "Go to his house. Ask him what he was thinking. Tell him how much he hurt you. Tell him you miss him. Work it out."

I tilted my head. When did my little sister start giving relationship advice? She was a fifteen-year-old freshman.

"What?" Her eyes widened. "You think I don't hear things? Do you think Mom and Dad don't have fights or argue or hurt each other?"

It was my turn to widen my eyes. "I know they get upset with each other sometimes, but no. They don't hurt each other."

"Yeah, they do. Not on purpose. But it happens." She held up a concealer stick. "Did you moisturize?"

I nodded but was still thinking about Mom and Dad hurting each other. That couldn't be true.

Madi dabbed a drop under each eye and patted it

into my skin. "You haven't been sleeping well. Your eyes tell on you."

"How do you know that about Mom and Dad?" I asked.

"I know lots of things. I talk to Mom about this stuff. You should too." She brushed a little blush onto my eyelids and my cheeks. "When are you getting another phone?"

I wanted to shrug or shake my head, but she had ahold of my chin, and I felt as if I couldn't move. "Whenever it comes in the mail. I don't know."

She released my chin, reached back to her makeup bag, and then held up the tube of lip gloss. "Talk to Roan today," she said with a bossy tone, giving me a pointed look.

I slipped the tube from her fingers but didn't answer. Madi left the bathroom to get her things. I applied the lip gloss and stuffed it into my pocket. My little sister had a talent for making me look good. As much as I hated to admit it, she gave good advice too.

The tightness in my chest lessened. Knowing I was going to talk to Roan hurt less than knowing I would never talk to him again. I knew what I had to do.

I knocked on Roan's front door. His truck wasn't in the drive, but that didn't always mean anything.

My sister was right. I needed to talk to him, but he wasn't anywhere to be found at school today. I could have sent him a message through Madi or Cayla, but I didn't want to do things that way.

We needed to be face to face. I wanted to see his expression. See if he was telling me the truth. Understand why he wanted to keep us a secret.

Marilyn opened the door. "Tommie, come on in." She stepped back, wearing an apron with flour smudged across it, and waved me in. "I'm making a pie," she said as she started toward the kitchen.

I stepped in and closed the door, following her. "When did you get back?" I asked. Did Roan say anything to them about me? Us?

"Oh, it was late Sunday. Jim's brother had to go back in for emergency surgery. He's not doing too well." She washed her hands at the kitchen sink, drying them on a hand towel. A partially rolled out pie crust lay on the countertop. She gripped the rolling pin and got back to her crust.

"I'm sorry to hear that. Is he going to be okay? Where's Jim?" Did he have to stay behind?

Roan stayed at home by himself for three weeks. Three weeks with me. Kissing me. Talking with me. Now we did none of the above.

"Jim's at his office, taking care of some things. Gerald, that's his brother's name, is not doing well. Did Roan tell you about our move?" she asked, pausing for my answer.

Um, we hadn't spoken since he went eleven rounds with my heart. I lost. Didn't know if my heart will recover. But the word *move* caused my stomach to knot. I didn't know why or what she even meant by it.

My eyebrows knit together. "What are you moving?"

Her expression softened. She straightened and wiped her hands on the apron. "I thought he would have told you when we first considered it. When he called after the game Saturday, we told him we would be moving to Florida."

My jaw dropped open. I think I stopped breathing too. Moving? To Florida?

"But..." I didn't know what to say. Roan mentioned downsizing, but I thought that meant a smaller house in Sweet Water. Why didn't he tell me? Was that why Roan never tried to talk to me again after Saturday? Did he think we were better off to end everything since he was moving?

Marilyn let out a huff. "That boy. He talks to you more than anyone and he didn't say a word about it?"

I shook my head, still too stunned and confused to say anything.

She sighed and turned back to her crust, gripping the handles of the pin. "He's a lot like his mother. God rest her soul. I loved that girl more than life itself. And Roan is like my own son. Even more special than that." Her eyes glazed over with moisture, and she blinked a few times.

"He is quiet and on the hard-headed side just like my Ashlyn was," she said and then shook her head. Marilyn was a strong woman. She didn't show a lot of emotion and rarely talked about her daughter. I guess it was easier for her that way.

My mind reeled, trying to understand what was happening. Questions mixed in and I had to ask before I got dizzy, "You're moving to Florida for good? Where will Roan live? When are you moving?"

"We'll be staying in Gerald's home until we know

what the future holds. He has a long recovery ahead of him, and since his wife passed last year, Jim is all he has. His kids live in different states and can't be there to help him out."

Was that what brothers and sisters did? My parents' families never had to deal with anything like that. Would my Mom have to move to help if her sisters needed care like that?

She rolled the crust onto the pin and gently transferred it to the pie plate. Sprinkling the counter with fresh flour, she continued, "We'll be leaving in a few weeks. We are considering renting this house." Marilyn unwrapped a ball of dough and flattened it on the counter, patting more flour on top of it and then doing the same with the rolling pin. "While Roan's at Tennessee meeting with the coach and players, he's supposed to see if he can get into a dorm early. We're not sure that will be an option."

"He can stay with us," I blurted out. It was the first thing that popped into my mind. He might have hurt me, but he had to have been hurting too, and I didn't even know it.

She stopped, mid-roll, and tilted her head at me. "I'm not sure about that. You have a house full the way it is, and your mother has a lot on her plate." She shook her head. "I don't know how she keeps up the way it is."

"Please. Let me talk to her. Just for the summer. Until he goes to college in the fall," I begged. Roan may not have even wanted to do it. He obviously didn't tell his grandparents we weren't friends anymore.

She pursed her lips for a moment. "I'll talk to Jim about it. Are you ready for graduation?" she asked. And just like that, she closed the door on that subject. She did that sometimes.

I hitched a shoulder. Cayla's mom was taking her to Hawaii right after the ceremony. Her mom was out of the picture most of the time, but at least Cayla had some perks to having a mom who worked for an airline. My dad would not make it home. I may not be able to share it with Roan. And if I didn't do something to get us back to at least being friends, graduation would be as depressing as a future without my best friend in it.

"Yeah, I guess." I watched her pour cherries mixed with flour and sugar into the dough and then sprinkle the top with cinnamon. "So when will Roan be back?"

Marilyn rolled the crust one last time, stopping to glance at me with a surprised expression. She shifted her weight, tilting her head and squinting as if she were watching a confusing play. Marilyn was a smart woman, intuitive. "He didn't tell you?"

I shook my head.

Her lips pressed into a thin line. She picked up the

knife off the counter and began cutting the crust into strips. "He should be back Friday night."

My heart squeezed. His future was becoming his present all too fast. How was I going to stop the divide between us? "Oh."

My throat tightened with disappointment and I didn't want her to know what was going on. If Roan left without us talking...no, I couldn't let that happen. If I didn't have a phone, I'd have to do it the old-fashioned way. Write him a note. "I think I left my bag and earbuds up in the media room. Do you mind if I look around?"

The knife sliced through the last strip. She glanced over, wearing a sweet smile, and said, "My home is your home, Tommie Sue. You've been part of this family since we moved in."

I smiled back. It was true. And I wasn't about to let it end now. I slipped off the bar stool, thanked her, and went upstairs.

The media room wasn't my destination though. I took a right down the hall. They had two master suites in this house. One downstairs, which his grandparents used, and Roan had the upstairs. It used to be his dad's— for the few years he lived here before moving back to Argentina. Roan took residence in it his freshman year.

I even helped him move his things. He kept the queen-sized bed. His grandparents had the room painted for him. He wanted green and gray, the school colors, but Marilyn wouldn't allow that. She said it was too drab and had it painted a sandy color.

Roan negotiated for sports memorabilia that hung on the walls. Baseball, of course. But he loved football too. He was good at everything.

I crossed the threshold and spotted the driftwood desk nestled in front of the window. He had left his laptop open, and I thought about opening a document to write my note on and leaving it up so he could see it.

When I stepped closer, I noticed his screen saver had changed. It used to be baseball photos and University of Tennessee logos, but now it was...me. My fingers covered my mouth as I watched the images slide across the screen, fading in and out. I didn't even remember some of them being taken.

There was one of us kissing in the rain. Where did he get that? An image of the lyrics to my favorite song faded in. My fingers fell to above my heart. I knew I often didn't read guys right, but this said I meant something more to him.

I watched selfies of the two of us fly by until I'd seen them all twice. My heart had worked itself up to a hopeful swell again. I slid out a sheet of paper from the desk drawer and grabbed a pen from the holder in the desktop's corner.

Roan wouldn't see it until tomorrow. I didn't know if I could handle that long of a wait, but it had already been a week. Whatever I wrote needed to be straight forward, like my dad said. If I wanted to save our friendship, I couldn't hold back.

"Roan..."

33

S ummer and I looked at each other across the table and slumped in our chairs at the same time. Cayla and Addison giggled, and I moved my gaze as if in a slumber to see what they were laughing at. They both had the same posture as Summer and me.

We both snickered.

"Ugh," Summer groaned, rubbing her belly. "I ate too much."

The words "Me too" popped up all around the table. Coach Hayes and Mac invited all the senior softball players to breakfast graduation morning. Addison, Summer, Mazzie, Cayla and I showed up. Veronica did too. I was thankful London didn't show her face.

"Sweet Water Stacks should come with a warning label," I said, waving my hand through the air as if it were written there. "Secret recipe contains ingredients that are highly addictive and could be hazardous to your hips."

That got a laugh from the entire table.

Coach Mac wagged a finger at me and said, "Jenkins, you were never that funny in practice. What's the deal? You're about to graduate and your personality changes?"

I shrugged. "Guess I was too worried about getting yelled at."

"I don't think that worked," Cayla said with a smirk.

"You weren't the only one," Summer said.

Throughout breakfast, Coach Hayes had given what she called "exit interviews" to each of the players. Only the pitchers were left, Mazzie and myself.

Veronica came back to the table. She took her seat and eyed Mazzie. "You're next," she said.

Mazzie swallowed, caught my eye, and wore an expression that seemed to mirror how I felt about having a one-on-one with Coach Hayes. My palms began to sweat, knowing I was next. Last.

I didn't want to think about it though, so I distracted myself and asked, "What is everyone doing today? Staying home? Going to the beach? A movie? We don't have to be at the football field until three o'clock."

Addison was the first to answer. "Sleep."

That got a few approvals.

"Sleep on the beach doesn't sound too bad," Summer

said. Her smile grew with a new thought. "A back row movie with Gabe sounds even better."

I tossed my napkin at her. "I'm so jealous of you two."

"Yeah," Cayla said. "You're too sweet to take on a pancake stomach."

Summer straightened, giggling, and pulled out her phone. Her grin widened as she said, "Speaking of sweet..."

The rest of the table groaned and threw their napkins too.

I wished we had this much fun during the season. Maybe they did, but I was too consumed with what happened at prom to enjoy anything. I had to stop allowing London or anyone else use that night to humiliate me. The one good thing that came out of it...the times I had kissed Roan.

Summer blocked the two napkins that flew close to her head. She smirked, lifted an eyebrow, and said, "Did y'all forget I'm the catcher?" She stood at the same time Mazzie came back.

Mazzie had sat on the chair next to Summer. Talking to Coach must not have been too painful, because Mazzie's bright blue eyes sparkled. "You're up," she said and sat down.

I sucked in a breath and leaned against Cayla sitting next to me. "It's fine," she whispered. "I promise."

I stood and stretched my spine for a second. Coach Hayes sat at a two-person table across the room of the restaurant. The place looked a lot like any other beachside breakfast diner. Light colors with an airy feel.

It wasn't likely Coach would gripe me out for anything since I was no longer a student at Sweet Water High. Hm. Did that make me an adult?

I crossed over the white and light blue checkerboard tile and took the seat every other softball player had sat in that morning. "Coach," I greeted.

"Tommie. How was your breakfast?" she asked, sipping a half-empty cup of coffee. Her gray eyes had a tendency to cut right through you. But she seemed different at the moment. Soft and gentle like a fluffy kitten.

The closed file folder on the tabletop had a stack of papers on top of it. I wondered what she had said to the other players. My hand rubbed at my belly. "It was good," I said. "I'm stuffed."

She grinned. The speech she and Coach Mac gave before our food arrived was nice. Nicer than they had been the whole season. They both wished the seniors the best of luck and offered to help us in any way they could for our future.

"Tommie, you had a lot of potential when the season began. I believed you would play a special part our team."

I ducked my head. That potential thing didn't work out so great.

"You stumbled for a bit and that stunted your growth. Life happens and sometimes," she snapped her fingers and waited for me to look at her before she continued, "Sometimes we can't control what other people do or what is happening around us. The one thing you can control is yourself."

My stomach tightened. It already hurt from the pancakes, but according to Cayla, Coach would not be chewing my butt this morning. I rubbed at my stomach again and tried to keep eye contact.

"You need to learn to control you, Tommie. Learn to focus and tune out the distractions. This will help you be successful not only when you play next year but also in your studies and future."

I pursed my lips and glanced down at the table. I said in a low voice, "I'm not playing next year."

She tilted her head. A smile played on her lips. "Do you want to play?" she asked.

"Yeah, of course." My eyebrows shot up and then knit together. I loved softball. I would miss some of these girls so much. "But I didn't have any offers. I'm not sure I could even walk on at Sweet Water College."

She straightened, shifting her back against the chair, and asked, "Did you know I was a walk-on my freshman year?"

I shook my head. Coach had played for Florida and had even made it onto the Olympic team before she injured her knee and ended her career. She was a tough coach, but I respected her. The whole team did.

She flipped through her papers and pulled out a sheet, glancing over it before she said, "I had an interesting conversation with the coach from the University of Tennessee yesterday."

I stared. I didn't know what she was getting at. Roan had a scholarship to play at UT, but why would the baseball coach be calling her?

"It seems someone has pointed you out to them. Made a strong argument on what an asset you would be to their team." Coach handed me the paper. "I agreed. They sent this to me."

It had the University of Tennessee and the softball coach's name at the top. I scanned the letter. When I came across my name, it caught my breath. I glanced at Coach. Her smile had stretched. She nodded for me to continue.

I continued reading. They offered me a partial scholarship to play next year. And based on performance, I could qualify for more the following year. My heart swelled inside my chest. I didn't know what to think or say.

"I...is this real? Did you tell them about me?" I asked. It caught me off guard because, well, let's face it, I got yelled at A LOT this last year. Not that I didn't deserve it, but I didn't think Coach thought I would be good enough to play for UT.

Her lips pursed for a second before she answered. "Yes, it's real. They are making you an offer. I'm sorry to say it wasn't me who talked to them. I believe it was a friend of yours."

The slight uptick in my heart rate inched higher. The only person I could think of was Roan. Why would he have done that when we weren't even talking? I left him a note, pouring my heart out, and he didn't come over when he got home last night or this morning.

I needed to confirm it though. "Roan Martin?" But how could he have any pull with the softball team?

"He must believe in you," she said. "Congratulations."

She went on about other things, but I didn't even hear the rest. I had a scholarship? With Roan's help. To the same college he was going to.

I had to find Roan.

34

"**D**o you see him?" I asked Cayla for the fifty-bazillionth time since we arrived at school for graduation. The chairs on the grass were already filled with family and loved ones here to watch the ceremony.

She gripped my shoulders and looked up at me. "Stop. His grandparents are already seated. Roan won't miss his own graduation."

I let out a frustrated groan. After we left Sweet Water Stacks, Cayla took me straight to Roan's house. He wasn't there. I asked Marilyn to send him a message I was looking for him and I didn't have a phone. He didn't reply to her. At least not while I was there.

My chest was so tight that one poke and I would have exploded. At the rate my heart was beating, it might burst first anyway. "What if I don't get to see him afterward?"

"Am I going to have to slap you in front of the entire class?" she asked, her voice in a harsh whisper. "He lives two houses away from you. Marilyn—"

"I know, but, ugh." I tried to breathe in a deep breath but a sharp pain in my chest wouldn't allow it. "I'm going to have a heart attack or stroke waiting."

Cayla tugged me down on the bench. "Think about something else. Like me lying on the beach in Hawaii, watching the hot surfers every day." She sighed, closing her eyes for a few moments. "I want Mom to do as much as possible. Who knows if I'll ever get the chance to go back?"

My anxious heart settled a little. "I'm excited for you. Jealous, but excited." A giggle bubbled out. It took me by surprise because I'd been so worried about where Roan was and hadn't been successful in finding him today.

"Send me a message when you get your phone so I can start sending you pictures," she said, swiping the green and gray tassel of her graduation hat out of her face. She glanced down at the gown I wore over my new dress. She shook her head and muttered, "Gray and green."

I tilted my head and scanned her matching robe. "It could be worse."

"Places, everyone," Miss Banks called our attention. She was so short, I didn't spot her, but her voice was big enough to cut through our noise.

All the seniors lined up as we had practiced earlier. Roan fit somewhere between Cayla and myself. I glanced back to see if he had slipped in. Still, he was nowhere to be found.

The two lines of students began moving, and I had to turn my attention to walking onto the football field.

When we approached the gate, the band played "Pomp and Circumstance." That was our cue to march onto the field, down the middle of the chairs set up, and take our assigned seats. I glanced at the chairs where Marilyn and Jim were sitting earlier. Mom, Brendan, and Madi were sitting next to them.

Roan had to be there, but when I glanced back at his row, I didn't see him. It took forever for the class to march to our seats. The JROTC presented the American flag, and Pastor Bryant gave the invocation.

As we sat, I turned to the row behind me across the aisle where Roan should have been. He was there. I stared at him, hoping he would look at me.

Roan's gaze met mine. His face was a blank slate, but his eyes bore into me.

I had tons of questions. I mouthed the first one that came out, "Where have you been?"

His expression softened. The corners of his lips lifted into a small smile. He didn't answer me, but he didn't look away either.

I watched him like that until I got a kink in my neck

and had to face forward again. My cap bumped the person's sitting next to me, Amber Justice. "Oops, sorry," I whispered. I didn't really know her. She wasn't into sports.

Amber lifted an eyebrow, straightening her cap. "What's your deal?" she asked.

I grimaced and shrugged.

Minutes felt like hours. I wished I hadn't lost my phone. No, I knew I had to do it face to face.

I shifted in my seat, picked at my nails, glanced at Roan, glanced at Cayla, tapped my toes, bounced my knees...

A hand gripped my wrist. Arlan, the kid that sat to my left, whispered, "Please stop. I can't take it anymore." His brown eyes pleaded with me. A bead of sweat streamed from his dark hair near his ear down his skin.

I leaned back against my chair, raising my hands in front of me. "Sorry," I whispered back.

The sun was sinking, but it had beat down on the field all day. Turf added at least fifteen degrees to the temperature. As much as I liked the heat, over one hundred degrees was just plain hot. It was a good thing Madi twisted my hair up. She did Cayla's too. I couldn't have imagined having my hair down like some girls.

The more time that ticked by the tighter my chest became. Cayla had calmed me down some before we marched onto the field, but being that close to Roan and not being able to talk to him was torturous.

Mrs. Parks announced Kaiya Surena as valedictorian. I glanced back at Roan again. He caught my eye and pointed to the stage, urging me to pay attention. I rolled my eyes and focused that direction.

Kaiya stood at the podium and greeted everyone like every other graduation I'd ever attended. I knew the ceremony was a rite of passage of sorts. But could it be any more boring? And long?

I hunched over, propped my forearms on my knees, and hoped for a breeze to swirl through my row. A shower was going to be in order after this. Steaks on the grill didn't even sound appealing. Or chocolate fudge cake with whipped cream icing. Ice cream, I could go for that.

Laughter erupted around me. I leaned back in my chair, glanced around, and up to the stage. The large screen scrolled images of school events from football games to our state baseball champions. The team got a rousing applause. Kaiya talked about change. How it was a constant in life. And that it can be hard even when we want it. Photos of seniors throughout the year faded in and out on the screen as she spoke.

Kaiya's words were so true to my life that year. It was as if she was talking directly to me.

She continued, "Sometimes we fail at change." A

picture of Roan with his arm draped around me in the lunchroom paused on the screen.

I froze, hoping the image of me fish-lipping James didn't show up.

"We want it so badly, but we screw it up. Maybe we are afraid to fail or afraid to succeed," she said as the photo changed to Roan and me. Both of us in our uniforms, smiling, holding hands with our gear bags over our shoulders.

My chest squeezed. I was ready to leave that part of Roan and me behind and go back to being friends. I didn't want to lose him. Now it was out in the open. Exactly what he didn't want. I glanced back at him with my mouth hanging open, ready to say something, but the words wouldn't come.

His deep-set amber eyes were soft. He pointed toward the screen.

I peeled my gaze away and looked at the screen again.

"Afraid to lose something we cherish when we realize our mistake." She paused and a photo of Roan holding a sign that said *I'm sorry* paused too. The crowd buzzed with chuckles. "We ask for forgiveness."

My hand went to my chest. I gripped the fabric of the gown. Was this part of the speech or was he apologizing to me? In public? I was about to turn to Roan when the screen changed.

"And hope to keep pressing forward for our own happily ever after," she ended.

A photo from Roan kissing me in the rain appeared. The words *Roan and Tommie 2019* were typed across the top of the image.

It knocked the breath out of me. My eyes widened. My heart whirled in my chest. Where did she get that?

Some students gasped along with me. Whoops and whistles erupted with applause.

I leaned back against the wooden slat of the folding chair to see Roan's expression. I had so many questions. The faces in the sea of gray and green were all honed in on me, but none were Roan's. I swallowed. Did he leave?

I tipped farther, balancing on the back two legs. The chair wobbled and threatened to crash in the row behind me.

A hand landed on my shoulder, steadying me. I turned to thank Amber. Only it wasn't her.

Roan stood before me, looking unsure, maybe even a little scared. His dark eyebrows arched over his golden eyes. A green tie peeked above the zipper of the gray gown. The drab color couldn't wash out his year-round tan. He reached for my hand.

Now that he stood so close to me, I was even more breathless than before. I placed my hand in his and stood. All the noise and people around us faded until I focused solely on Roan.

"I'm sorry," he said and moved closer.

"This was you?" I asked, still not sure if it was Kaiya pranking the sloppy kisser from prom or him really asking for forgiveness for hurting me.

He nodded and then tilted his head. "Well, Kaiya helped me out." His expression turned serious. He leaned as close as he could without our caps banging against each other's. "I got your note."

I nodded.

"You were right. I wanted to keep us a secret. And James likes you too. I—" He paused and swallowed. "I backed off for baseball so we would have a better chance to win state. I'm sorry. I know we have a lot to talk about, but...I hope this—" he waved toward the stage— "makes up for some of it. It's not a secret anymore. I like you a lot, Toms, and I messed up. Is it too late for us?" he asked, gripping my waist.

Knowing hundreds of eyes were on us should have freaked me out, but that was only a tiny reason that my heart pounded in my chest. Roan wanted the "us" we had become. There was no denying it to James or the baseball team or anyone else.

His throat bobbed. The surrounding noise continued, and so did he. "I want us to be together. I need you, Toms." His voice cracked, revealing his heart.

I was speechless. The way he said he needed me, broken and full of emotion, prompted a sheen of tears to cover my eyes. A smile stretched across my lips, along with a nervous giggle. I wanted to kiss him, touch those beautiful lips to mine, but I didn't want to push him. I slid my arms around his waist and said, "I've missed you."

"Are you going to kiss her or what?" Gabe's voice rang out above the buzz of the crowd.

Roan rolled his eyes.

"Kiss her already," Cayla shouted.

I was sure I heard Summer and a few others start up a chant that grew. "Kiss. Kiss. Kiss."

An authoritative voice grumbled something, but I was so focused on Roan's kiss-me-eyes, I couldn't focus on anything else.

Amber bumped his arm and said, "Kiss her while you have the chance."

Roan's full lips flashed a grin. He pulled his cap off and dipped his head, pressing his lips to mine. His arms encircled me, pulling me close.

The sparks from his lips ignited a warmth inside that made me want to melt against him. My fingers grasped his gown and then slid up his shoulders, to the back of his neck, and found their way into his thick dark hair. For however long the moment was, time stood still.

The kiss chant turned into hoots and whistles from our surrounding classmates.

"Mr. Martin," Mrs. Parks barked through the microphone. "Please take your seat. The graduation ceremony is not over yet." She wasn't happy about the interruption.

I was though. Embarrassed? Yeah, but not humiliated like the prom kiss. I don't think I had ever been happier in my life.

Roan, the kissing tutor.

My boyfriend.

35

"Tommie," Mom called to me from the kitchen. "Your daddy's on the phone for you."

I was in the middle of unboxing my phone replacement. It delivered right before I left for graduation. I handed it to Roan, who was beside me on the sofa with Juju on his lap, petting her. "I'll be back."

He grinned, taking the box and placing it on the cushion beside him. "I can set it up for you," he said.

After we got back from graduation, Roan's family agreed to join us for burgers instead of going out to dinner.

"Okay," I agreed and squeezed his hand. "Thanks."

I tracked across the subfloor of the living room to the kitchen. Mom finished removing the wall between the two rooms. The drywall was up and painted. All she had left was the flooring.

"Here she is," Mom said into her cell phone. "I love you, baby." She handed it to me. Mom's smile was a lot like Madi's and mine. I wondered if I would look like her when I got older. That wouldn't be a bad thing. She was pretty and stayed fit with all the hours she worked and put into remodeling.

I slipped the phone from her hand and placed it next to my ear. "Hello?"

"Congratulations, Tommie girl," Dad said as if he was the announcer at a wrestling match.

I giggled. "Thanks."

"I heard you got in a bit of trouble in the middle of the ceremony. Want to tell me about it?"

I coughed, nearly choking on my spit. "I, uh…" I stumbled over the words and travelled away from the adults back toward Roan. Not that I didn't think Mom would tell Dad what happened. I wasn't prepared for the question right off the bat. "So you heard?" I asked, buying time.

"I heard, but I'd like to debrief you on the situation." An engine hummed in the background.

Juju trotted past me toward the kitchen as I came to a stop in front of Roan.

He glanced at me from his project of setting up my phone.

I gave him a pleading look and held my hand out for him to take it, nodding toward the stairs.

Dad might be teasing, but sometimes it was hard to tell. I replied the best I could, "Dad. I think that's overkill."

Roan gathered the phone and box and stood, sliding his hand in mine.

Dad chuckled. "Maybe. So Roan was the boy you asked for advice on?"

Roan and I stepped to the stairs and made our way to my bedroom.

"Yeah," I answered my dad. "Being honest about feelings is a lot harder than it sounds." It was something Roan and I needed to work on. Because I didn't want to go through something like that again.

"It is. Usually the hard things are worth it. I want to talk more about the two of you, but I don't a lot of time. I hear he might be staying at the house this summer?"

"Maybe." I tried to explain the problem. Roan took a seat on the floor and I sat cross-legged, mirroring him. "His grandparents are moving to Florida, but they're not sure what they will do with the house."

"Not sure I like that idea since—" Men's voices carried through the airwaves from the background, cutting his words. Dad was quiet as if he were listening. He gave a muffled response before returning to me.

"Sorry about that, kiddo. Where was I? Oh, a scholarship? How do you feel about that?" he asked.

I looked at Roan, who had released my hand and

turned his attention back to my phone. The offer was a total surprise and left me unsure of what to do. "It's not a full ride or anything. I think I might try. It's quite a ways from home, but Roan will be there. So I won't be alone. What do you think I should do?"

"I'm not sure about you and Roan being out there together. I know you two have been close friends since he moved down the road, but..." He paused. I thought I heard him sniff. "You're my little girl. I don't like to think about you growing up like that."

My chin quivered, and tears immediately welled up. "It's okay, Dad." My voice wavered a bit.

Roan caught my gaze. His brow furrowed, and he reached for my cheek, wiping a tear with his thumb. His hand slid across my shoulder and down my arm, lifting my hand to his lips.

That put a grin on both our faces. Roan kept my hand tucked in his while he went back to setting up my phone.

Dad cleared his throat. "You should go. Live life. You be the strong young woman I know your mother has taught you to be."

"Yes, sir," I said, swallowing down my tears. "I will do my best to do that."

"I don't want to, but I need to hang up. What do you say I take my leave so I can move you to college?" he asked.

I straightened, surprised he would want to do that. "That would be great. Do you think you could?"

"You know I can't promise, sweetie, but I'll do my best." He was owned by the Marines, whether he liked it or not.

Even though I knew that, it didn't make it easier. "Yeah, I know. I love you, Dad. Thanks for calling."

The hum of the engine quieted and voices sounded again. "I'm proud of you. I love you, Tommie girl. Bye, now."

"Bye," I said, though I think he might have hung up already.

I pulled the phone away from my ear and stared at the screen. Dad was gone. At least I got to talk to him on graduation.

"You okay?" Roan asked.

I looked up from the phone in my hand and nodded. "Yeah. He didn't give me too much grief about you. Probably because he didn't have much time to talk."

Roan shrugged. "He has plenty of time to get used to it. It's not like I'm some guy he knows nothing about. I'm not a panty stealer."

My eyes widened. "What?" I asked with a giggle.

He chuckled too. "You're the only one for me. I tried to make that clear today."

I dipped my head. It almost didn't seem real...Roan and me.

He let loose of my hand and lifted my chin with his finger. "I know I screwed up. I was a coward and scared and didn't know what my grandparents moving would mean for us. I should have told you, but..."

I leaned over and kissed his cheek. "You weren't the only one who made mistakes. I was desperate to replace my public prom kiss humiliation with a worthy public kiss so I wouldn't look like an idiot anymore. I didn't consider what you wanted."

"It was worth Mrs. Parks yelling at us," he said with a smirk.

I leaned over and placed my palm on his chest above his heart. "Thank you. For doing all that today."

He placed his hand on top of mine and whispered, "You're worth it."

"Ugh," Brendan grumbled, leaning against the frame of my door. "I don't know if I'll be able to get used to mushy couple stuff from you two."

I stood, Mom's phone in one hand, and reached for Roan. He stood and slid his fingers through mine. "You'll figure it out," I said.

Brendan stuffed his hands in his shorts pockets. "You're going to the beach party, right?" he asked.

"Yeah," Roan said. "We need to finish your phone, Toms, then head out."

"Are you going?" I asked my brother. "I thought it was for seniors."

"Sometimes those who graduated already go. I might. I don't know." He shrugged. "I assume Cayla's going? All your friends?"

I glanced at Roan. He grinned. We might have picked up on Brendan's motive.

"Cayla left for Hawaii right after graduation. She won't be back for two weeks."

Brendan's face flashed disappointment, but he quickly masked it. "Wish Mom and Dad would have sent me to Hawaii for two weeks after graduation."

Roan released my hand and crossed the room to my desk, opening my laptop.

"Maybe we'll see you at the party?" I asked.

Brendan watched Roan for a second and then looked at me. He gave me a soft smile. "Yeah, maybe." He pulled me into a quick hug and said, "I'm happy for you."

"Thanks," I whispered.

He walked out of my room, and I turned to watch Roan.

For the first time in months, I was eager to go to the party. Roan said he had a special playlist but wouldn't give up any details.

After graduation, the hugs and congratulations about my new boyfriend came from Cayla, Summer, Gabe, and so many people I couldn't believe. Even James congratulated me. Or something like that. It felt like he had more he wanted to say, but he backed away without finishing it.

Roan said he got the photo of us kissing in the rain from James. I guess James knew about us for a while.

We still had things to talk about, but for the moment, a bonfire graduation party was on our minds.

36

Whe Roan and I walked up to the bonfire, the stares from our teammates, at least the ones I could see, landed on our clasped hands. Summer shot across the crowd like a fastball.

"Hi," she said with a quick wave. It was more to Roan than me.

Jenna followed behind her, greeting us by wiggling her fingers.

"Um," Summer uttered, reaching between Roan and me. She snagged my arm and tugged me in the opposite direction. "You don't mind if we steal Tommie for a bit, do you?"

It must not have been an actual question because Summer didn't wait around for an answer. Jenna looped her arm through mine too. Teammates on either side of me.

"I..." I started, but Jenna shushed me. My neck craned as I kept my gaze on Roan, not wanting to be separated from him. He stood there, the strap of our chairs slung over his shoulder, and a cooler in one hand, looking as stunned as I felt.

They were in such a rush, guiding me around the bonfire, through the sand, and toward the ocean, that I lost a shoe.

"Wait," I said, resisting their efforts. "My flip-flop."

They stopped. While Jenna let go of my arm long enough to run back for it, I asked, "What are you guys doing?"

"So, when did you and Roan become a thing?" Summer asked.

"Girl," Jenna drawled out before I could answer Summer. "I almost fell up out of my chair when I saw those pictures today."

I giggled. My happy bucket overflowed. This was the kind of attention I didn't mind. It was so weird to talk openly about Roan as my boyfriend. "You weren't the only one."

Summer gasped. "So you didn't know all that was going down?"

I shook my head. "Nope." The light in the sky was fading, causing the ocean to look like a dark abyss.

We stopped in front of the water, plopping our butts in the sand. Jenna handed over my other shoe. I slipped my other one off, placing them in front of me so I could dig my toes into the warmth that was clinging to the sand.

Jenna and Summer put me through a rapid-fire barrage of questions before we made it back to the fire. Music played from somewhere nearby. We stopped at the edge of the crowd when we saw a few of our teammates.

The fire burned bright with red and blue flames. Between it and the song playing, they hypnotized me for a moment. I maneuvered closer to the warmth.

There were a lot more people than when we first arrived. Some were dancing nearby. Even couples. All faces I recognized from school. My senior class. I couldn't believe only four years ago, I was a freshman. Now I was basically an adult leaving for college soon. Mom and Dad were right—it went by so fast. I was glad to leave the high school drama behind though.

I scanned the crowd for Roan. Lucas Addington and Charlotte Robinson had their arms around each other, talking as if no one was around. Ky Andrews wasn't far away with his girlfriend, Emmy. Oh, Wes Schultz was here too. Lauren was by his side. They seemed to be the royal couple of Sweet Water.

Oh, my gosh. Jett Bryant and Harper Tisdale were so adorable. They picked us up in his ATVs at the parking area when we arrived. He let Roan drive one, and I was on behind him. My arms were wrapped around him so there was no space between us.

Carson Brooks was talking animatedly. Mia Randalls was laughing next to him. She changed a lot this year. It was probably because of Carson. They were opposites.

Seeing these guys in the crowd...they were all on my Top Hot Guys of Sweet Water list. Bentley Nelson was here with his new girlfriend, Bailey Garber. Even Jeremy Dermot and Sydney Thane were here.

I giggled to myself. At the crazy idea my sister and best friend came up with. The kissing tutor. It was so ridiculous. Roan was right about that. In the end, I got the guy. The one that was right for me.

I continued searching for Roan. James Lowe caught my eye. He stood near Jason Hunt and Amber Kelley. She played volleyball with my sister. Other football players gathered nearby, moving from group to group. Roan played football, but baseball was always his favorite.

Close by James was Gabe Washington and some baseball players. I spotted Roan across the fire, parked in one of the beach chairs we had brought.

Just the sight of him caused a quiver in my chest, and a smile lifted my lips. He already wore his sweet grin. I wondered if he had been watching me.

The warm glow of the fire danced on his face, making him more handsome. I almost sighed out loud at the sight of him. This had been the best day of my life. Roan made my life better. Period.

I tilted my head and watched him watching me. It was hard to do. My heart pounded louder with every second that ticked by because things were different for us. Better.

My favorite song came on. Roan mentioned something about making a playlist for tonight. Did he do this? My smile widened, remembering how he wanted me to think of him every time I heard it. The way he kissed me. I swallowed. It totally worked because I was remembering the way his lips tasted.

That beautiful grin of his widened. His mouth began to move. At first, I thought he was telling me something but soon realized he was singing the lyrics to me. He lifted his chin as if he wanted me to sit next to him.

My heart melted and the need to touch him, kiss him, was strong. I didn't know if I could resist. Instead of marching over there, I dug my toes into the sand. I wanted him to come to me.

He stood, parted the sea of people between us, and made his way to me. Just like the song. Our eyes never left each other's. The quiver in my stomach had expanded to my chest.

When he reached me, he grasped my hand, pressed his other against my waist, gave me a quick kiss on the lips, and spun me around.

I gasped. The flip-flops I'd been holding slipped through my fingers, landing on the ground a few feet from us.

Our entwined hands crossed my body and rested on my hip. He nestled close to me so that my back was pressed against his chest and his free hand was on my other hip, guiding my movements.

We had danced like this before. When a school dance was coming up, he gave me a few lessons. It always ended with him stopping abruptly and walking away in a huff. Maybe the problem wasn't that I was bad. It could have been he liked it more than he thought he should.

He moved us to the beat of the song in a slow salsa mix. Roan knew what he was doing. I followed his lead.

I craned my neck to ask, "I thought you didn't dance in public?"

His lips dipped down to my neck and kissed me through my hair, and answered, "I didn't do a lot of things before today. It's kind of freeing." His fingers grazed my skin as he brushed my hair from my neck.

"Besides," he hummed, "you look amazing in that dress. I couldn't resist."

My heart soared. I didn't want to resist. The way his body molded to mine was so natural and easy. How much more could my heart take? It felt like it would burst at any moment, and we had plenty of night to go.

Roan's fingers pressed against my hip before he spun

me away and brought me back face to face. One hand continued to hold mine while the other gripped my hip and brought me closer. He stepped back with one foot and I followed. Our bodies were in sync. Every step, he inched us closer and closer.

He released my fingers, placed my hand on his shoulder, and slid his around my waist.

Every touch left goosebumps in its wake. My eyes were as wide as could be. I loved every second of it but was surprised he would do this anywhere other than a dance studio or his house.

I knew others found him intimidating. Not me. Until he set his attention, his focus, all on me. I held my breath. It was... beautiful. "Roan," I breathed.

He pressed his forehead to mine. "Tommie Sue," he answered in a low, raspy voice. His lips meet mine in a rush.

Howls and whistles erupted around us.

Roan's lips moved across my cheek to my ear. "Can we take a walk? I can't kiss you like I want in front of all these people."

I bit my lip, holding in the emotion from the day that was hitting me right in the heart. "Yes, please," I squeaked out.

We weaved through a few people and slipped away until there was nothing but sand, crashing waves, salty ocean breeze, and us.

EPILOGUE

"Tommie girl, I can't believe you're old enough to leave the nest," Dad said, hugging me again. He gave the best hugs, but he had done it so many times the past two days, I think my ribs were bruised.

The truck door shut, signaling Roan had everything packed for our trip.

"Thanks for helping me move," I said, pulling away. "For coming home. I missed you."

Dad's eyes shined with moisture. He rubbed my shoulder and said, "I missed you too. Are you sure you don't want me to drive you to school?"

I chuckled and shook my head. "No, Dad. I think Roan can handle it."

Dad grunted and focused a stern look at Roan.

Jim and Marilyn took turns hugging Roan. They had returned from Florida to see him off. Jim said, "You two make sure to come see us during Christmas break." He broke off from Roan and hugged me too. "I have two round trip tickets with your names on them," he said.

Marilyn reached for me and wrapped her arms around me. "That's right," she said. "And we'll be up to see one of your games. Both of you."

I nodded and released her. "Thank you. For everything."

Marilyn and Jim sold their house down the street from mine. They said it was too big for one person to live in but allowed Roan to stay the summer at my house. They said when we graduate from college, they'll put a down payment on a house in Sweet Water if we plan to move back full-time.

She patted my cheek. "Thanks for taking care of our boy. You're good for each other."

My smile widened. I didn't know what she would think of Roan and me being together as a couple. I wasn't exactly high-end girlfriend material. But thanks to Madi, I learned some fashion sense and how to dress for my body. I still hated shopping though. I planned to save all that for when I came home for visits.

I stepped toward Madi. She stood there with her perfect golden hair pulled into a ponytail, holding Juju. Sweat beaded at the edge of my sister's hairline, sporting a flushed face. She held our black Pug close while her lips pressed tightly together, but it couldn't hide their quiver.

"Coach tried to kill you this morning?" I asked, teasing to ease the tightness in my throat. I took Juju out of her arms and tucked her close to my side.

Madi nodded about her practice and a tear spilled over her light brown lashes.

That was all it took for mine to do the same. She rushed at me and flung her arms around me.

"I'm so glad we became friends," I whispered.

Roan and everyone talked in the background. It was another perfectly sunny morning in Sweet Water, North Carolina. Perfectly hot and humid too. Living near the mountains was going to be a new experience. One of so many that lie ahead of us.

Madi sniffed and said, "Me too." She took in a heavy breath. "I want to come see you some time. Okay?"

"Of course," I said. "Any time."

"You two are too much," Mom said, embracing us both. "I wasn't going to cry."

Madi and I laughed.

Brendan joined us on the other side of Mom. "What's going on?" he asked. "Secret girl meeting?"

We giggled and broke apart. I gave him a solo hug too. He was my brother, after all. "Something like that," I said.

"Have fun, sis," he mumbled against my shoulder.

"But don't screw up your grades, okay? Promise me you'll study and graduate."

Brendan had been as lost as me, trying to find his way after high school. He took last year off and worked at Sweet Surf. He decided to join the Marines. He didn't want to leave his boss hanging, so he chose a date that was after the big surfing season to leave for boot camp. I didn't know if I'd see him before then or not.

"I will. I promise. I love you. I'm proud of you for taking a year off and for not rushing in to join just because Dad did."

"Thanks. Love you too," he said and stepped back. "Roan." They shook hands and did a quick hug. "Take care, man. See you sometime."

"I want to be there for your boot camp graduation. If I can make it work." Roan glanced at me. "I'll make sure Tommie's there."

Brendan nodded. "Don't forget what I said."

Roan rubbed his lips together, doing his best not to grin too big. He nodded and said, "It won't be a problem."

Dad moved toward Roan and Brendan. His blue plaid shirt made his eyes a brighter blue than usual. I imagined it was quite a change from his desert cami's. He put his hand on Brendan's shoulder. "Did we have the same conversation?"

Any hint of a grin Roan had on his face left when

Dad stepped in. He answered, "Pretty close to the same. Yes, sir. You have nothing to worry about."

"Sweetie," Mom said, drawing my attention away from the testosterone show. "Do you have your schedule and room key? Did you pack pads and tampons? I'd hate for you to start and not be prepared."

Heat burned my cheeks. "Mom," I hissed. "Not in front of the guys. Geesh."

"Oh, Tommie, they know all about these things. If Roan doesn't, you should educate him."

I rolled my eyes. I'm sure it was just as embarrassing for Dad and my brother as it was for me. "I have everything." I hugged her for the last time. "I love you. I'll let you know when we get there."

I kissed Juju on top of her head and squeezed her one last time. "I love you too, girl."

She whimpered.

"I'm going to miss you, but sissy said she'd take good care of you." I pet her dark coat one last time and handed her over to Madi. A tear slipped out of the corner of my eye. Juju's kept me company through good times and bad. She's family too.

I hurried to Roan, slipped my hand in his, and tugged him toward the truck.

"Don't forget to call when you get there," Mom said.

"Let me know too," Madi added.

Brendan waved. "Me too," he said.

"Roan," Marilyn called, "let us know too."

Roan opened my door as he nodded. "I will."

I stepped onto the step board and turned back. "I'll send a group message to everyone. Love y'all." I slid into the smooth leather seat and Roan closed the door.

I took a deep breath and was letting it out when Roan got in the driver's side. "Just a bit overwhelming, huh?" he said.

I grunted a laugh. "Yeah, just a bit."

The truck was backed into my drive to load the last of my things earlier. He shifted into gear and we pulled out onto the street. Roan honked. We waved at everyone still gathered on the concrete by the house as we pulled away.

"I'm exhausted already," he said.

I slid my hand in his, finding some calm in his touch. "Tell me about it." I angle in my seat and asked, "What was all that with Brendan and Dad?"

"Basically, your dad reminded me he's a trained killer."

I gasped. "He did not."

He nodded with a grim expression. "Brendan said he's soon to be a trained killer and that I've caused you to cry enough already. Not to do it again."

"Oh, my gosh." I busted out laughing. "You know they'd never lay a finger on you."

"Maybe," he said with a shrug. "I don't plan on finding out."

We drove through Sweet Water and stopped at the stop sign before we turned on the highway.

Roan gave my fingers a squeeze and turned to look at me. "Are you ready for the first day of the rest of our lives?" he asked.

My smile widened. We were off on our own adventure. One that had my belly jittery with the nerves and excitement. "Yes. Absolutely."

Seven-and-a-half hours, two bathroom stops, and one lunch break later, we arrived at our destination. Sweet Water wasn't what I considered a small town, but compared to Knoxville, Tennessee, it was tiny. Luckily, I only had to be concerned with the campus. I doubted I would ever go off campus unless it was for softball or I was with Roan.

He pulled into the parking lot for my dorm and found a spot. The sun cast a warm glow on everything in its path. It made the campus more inviting. And I needed that because knots tried to weave together in my stomach. I had never been away from home before. Not like this.

Roan shut the truck off, unbuckled his seatbelt, and swiveled to face me. His tender golden eyes flickered with mischief.

I loved the way he grinned like that. His perfectly

white teeth peeked through the small separation of his lips, and one corner of his mouth lifted higher than the other. I didn't know why he was staring at me like that. It made my stomach tremble, and I giggled. "What?"

His eyes danced with excitement or maybe nerves. He said, "I haven't said anything, but I feel like this is the second chapter of us."

I clicked the button to release my seatbelt, leaned over the console, and thanked him for such a beautiful thing to say. After a long, delicious kiss, I decided I better stop before I got carried away the first official day on campus.

I sighed. "Love your idea. Our story. How many chapters do you think we'll have?" I stayed perched across the console, looking into his mesmerizing eyes.

"Hm," he sounded, pursing his lips. "What do you think?" he asked.

"I don't know. I hope a lot."

A brilliant smile stretched on his lips. He traced a thumb across my cheek. "I think our novel will be longer than *War and Peace*. Full of love and adventure, and since it's a true story...pain. But I've had enough of that in my life. I hope we don't have to deal with too much more. As long as we're on the same page together, our love will last until the end of our time."

Happy tears pooled along my lashes. My heart, my body, my mind was melting. I slid my hands over his shoulders, pulled him as close as possible, and pressed my lips to his with an appreciation I'd never felt before. He was beautiful. He thought I was beautiful. And he was mine. We were each other's. He split my heart wide open and took up residence.

I knew in that moment that one day we would marry each other. We had the best of both worlds: best friends and forever love.

But that day, that moment, was when our true love began.

Thank you for reading Tommie and Roan's story...the final installment of the Sweet Water High series.

Start from the beginning, and read the first book in the
Sweet Water High series
Misunderstanding The Billionaire's Heir
by Anne-Marie Meyer
https://amzn.to/2lpubFs.

LOVE SALLY'S WRITING AND WANT TO KNOW MORE? Join Sally's Notes https://www.subscribepage.com/BB. JoinSally'sNotes to get updates, musings, reading opportunities, and insider information.

DON'T FORGET TO LEAVE A REVIEW! LET OTHERS know how this book made you feel. 😍

LEAVE A REVIEW

If you enjoyed The Kissing Tutor, it would be a HUGE help if you leave a review.

Reviews help other readers see this book is worth their time.

THANK YOU

ACKNOWLEDGMENTS

Humbly, I give thanks to my Lord and Savior Jesus Christ, for Your permission to write and for all the people You sent to support and contribute to this project.

Thanks to you, for reading this story. I hope you've fallen in love with these characters as much as I have.

Kristyn Pearson...you're the best.

Kelsie Stelting, not only are you a fantastic writer, you're a great freind.

To my beta readers, Amanda and Vanessa, you always find time for my stories. Thank you!

Mom, Dad, and my family, thanks for your unconditional love and support.

A special thank you to my kids. Your love, excitement, and support mean so much to me. I love you 🫂

ABOUT THE AUTHOR

Hi! I'm Sally.

I grew up in the rural Midwest wandering through the woods and creeks of the countryside. Might have been a tomby like Tommie when I was a little girl. Hey, with three brothers, what do you expect?

That experience has been a tremendous influence on my writing, lending credibility to the voice of my characters. I combine the ingredients of reality with a dreamer's imagination to create sweet and delectable fiction.

Want to interact with me in real time? I have a private reader group on Facebook ... Regan Stone Readers.

I'm on Instagram of Facebook too!

THE TALK

When Roan's character first came to me, he was a lot different. His family history was going to be his grandparents were from Argentina and moved to America to extend the family business. Roan's parents were both going to be from Argentina and have strict family rules about dating and marrying from an approved/select family that were wealthy.

As the story evolved, Roan's background evolved too. His mother dying at a young age. His father, too distraught to stick around and face her memory all the time, moved back to his home country. That left Roan, alone, with his mother's parents. It would be tough to loose both your parents at a young age like that.

But Tommie girl was there for him. She was always there for him.

And having someone for you like that...you never forget it.

Roan might have screwed up, but it didn't take long for him to come to his senses.

You know what, he was there for Tommie through the years too. And I loved what Roan said, "I think our novel will be longer than *War and Peace*. Full of love and adventure, and since it's a true story...pain. But I've had enough of that in my life. I hope we don't have to deal with too much more. As long as we're on the same page together, our love will last until the end of our time."

Sigh.

Can you picture this tall, strong guy, dark honey skin, shaggy hair with a bit of waviness, and warm caramel-colored eyes saying this?

Double sigh.

I hope you enjoyed reading The Kissing Tutor as much as I enjoyed writing it.

Made in the USA
Middletown, DE
04 February 2021